VIRAGO MODERN CLASSICS
283

Nell Dunn was born in London in 1936, and educated at a convent until the age of 14, when she left without taking any exams. While living in Battersea and working in a sweet factory in her twenties, she began writing short stories about life in South London. She came to fame in 1963, when these short stories were collected and published as *Up the Junction*, which won the John Llewellyn Rhys Prize and was filmed for both television and cinema, becoming a controversial success. Her second novel, *Poor Cow*, was published in 1967; it was an instant bestseller and was adapted into a film by Ken Loach with Carol White and Terence Stamp. As well as her novels, Dunn has also written plays, collections of conversations and television scripts throughout her life.

Nell Dunn has three sons. She lives in London with two dachshunds.

Also by Nell Dunn

Up the Junction
The Incurable
I Want
Tear His Head Off His Shoulders
Living Like I Do
The Only Child
Grandmothers
My Silver Shoes

POOR COW

NELL DUNN

Introduction by Margaret Drabble

**A VIRAGO
MODERN CLASSIC**

VIRAGO

First published in Great Britain in 1967 by Mac Gibbon & Kee Ltd
First published in 1988 by Virago Press
This edition published in 2026 by Virago Press

1 3 5 7 9 10 8 6 4 2

Copyright © Nell Dunn 1967
Introduction copyright © Margaret Drabble 1988
Preface copyright © Nell Dunn 2013

The moral right of the author has been asserted.

*All characters and events in this publication, other than those
clearly in the public domain, are fictitious and any resemblance
to real persons, living or dead, is purely coincidental.*

All rights reserved.
No part of this publication may be reproduced, stored in a
retrieval system, or transmitted in any form or by any means, without
the prior permission in writing of the publisher, nor be otherwise circulated
in any form of binding or cover other than that in which it is published
and without a similar condition including this condition being
imposed on the subsequent purchaser.

A CIP catalogue record for this book
is available from the British Library.

ISBN 978-0-349-02085-3

Typeset in Goudy by M Rules
Printed and bound in Great Britain by
Clays Ltd, Elcograf S.p.A.

Papers used by Virago are from well-managed forests
and other responsible sources.

Virago Press
An imprint of
Little, Brown Book Group
Carmelite House
50 Victoria Embankment
London EC4Y 0DZ

The authorised representative
in the EEA is
Hachette Ireland
8 Castlecourt Centre
Dublin 15, D15 XTP3, Ireland
(email: info@hbgi.ie)

An Hachette UK Company
www.hachette.co.uk

www.virago.co.uk

FOR REUBEN

Let him kiss me with the kisses of his mouth:
for thy love is better than wine.

SONG OF SOLOMON

Contents

Preface: Memories of Battersea by *Nell Dunn*   ix
Introduction by *Margaret Drabble*   xiii

Poor Cow	1
In the Money	4
Trouble	10
Auntie Emm's	14
Love	25
More Trouble	38
Turned On	56
The Model	69
Joy Takes the Test	74
Memories	84

Still Dreaming	94
Tom Comes Out	104
Desolation	117

Preface by the author:
Memories of Battersea

I went to live in Battersea in 1959. The house was a two-storey cottage near a stream running into the Wandle, and in the back garden were an apple tree and a pear tree – the remains of the market garden it once was. The next-door family kept hens. The old mother lived downstairs and her children and grandchildren upstairs, and whenever they had a row the old lady locked her door and they couldn't get to the toilet which was out the back, so they had to come in to use mine. I had the only bath in the street so there was always a queue for it because my friends opposite had to fill a plastic bowl with water from the kitchen tap and then take it up to the tiny back bedroom they shared to wash. You washed your feet last because that was the dirtiest part of your body.

I loved Battersea. It was built on a hill and tumbled down the hill cottages and factories and the power station with its early morning plumes of mauve smoke drifting up into an early morning sky. In a side street half hidden in a doorway would stand the bookie in the evening darkness. Calling out to you in a low voice as you went by. Betting was illegal then. Abortion was illegal too, but names were passed around and many young women ended up in the local hospital with perforated wombs.

I loved the dogs. Stray dogs everywhere, and when my little brown bitch from Battersea Dogs Home came in season I would be followed by a great crowd of dogs till I had to run home and bang the door shut. In the summer evenings people hung about outside smoking, chatting and eating fish and chips. There were always a few stray dogs in the street and I saved bones and bacon rind for them. There were still a lot of bomb sites, and my two-year-old son would be taken by the big girls and boys to play king of the castle on the mounds of building debris. The women really ruled the roost in those days. Sometimes a man had to change his name to the woman's to fit in with the family.

In the morning the young women would go singing down the road to work, stopping at the bakers to buy fresh rolls to eat as they walked along. If they lost their job in one factory through cheek or pilfering they could get a job in another the next day. It was the same with boyfriends. There were so many factories: the butter factory, the sweet factory (where I worked), the button factory, the candle factory, the sugar factory and the brewery which smelt of sweet yeast, and babies left out in their prams, dummies stuck firmly between pink gums, would get covered with a thin sticky treacle And, in hot weather, flies.

The night of Princess Margaret's wedding everyone got drunk. The pubs were open till midnight and everyone got drunk and fought. It wasn't unusual for girls to fight over a man. Swinging each other around by the hair and screaming.

I bought my first pair of tight white jeans off a rail in the market, bleached my hair blonde, and wore it in a beehive. I was a writer when I went to live in Battersea but it took a long time to get published. In 1963 Karl Miller, the literary editor of the *New Statesman*, began to publish my stories, four of which are included in *Up the Junction*. He also showed me how to edit. How to pare them down to the lean, simple language that suited them. It was very thrilling to be published in the *New Statesman*.

Then I met Joy. She was standing outside her house in her bedroom slippers. She had thin white legs and pale gold hair. We became close friends and we still are close friends. After meeting her I wrote *Poor Cow*. Most of what I wrote in *Up the Junction* I heard; some of it I made up. *Poor Cow* was more a mixture of Joy and what happened to her, and also what happened to me. She had a caravan at Selsey Bill and we would go for the weekend and have a lovely time. I wrote about this in *My Silver Shoes*. I was happy when I was with Joy.

It all ended when the sanitary inspector came round and found silverfish under the lino. The house was declared unfit for human habitation, which was of course rubbish, and demolished. Battersea became full of derelict building sites and then, thanks to the town planners, concrete high-rise prison flats. I wrote *Up the Junction* and *Poor Cow* when I was still young enough to believe I was immortal. Life and its thrills were never going to end. Now, rereading these books I remember the excitement of escaping my unpeopled background to the energy of the city. I hope these books capture my time there – when the day began around six, eating fresh rolls on the way to work, and often ended after midnight kissing somewhere forbidden, someone forbidden.

Nell Dunn, January 2013

Introduction

Poor Cow, published in 1967, was Nell Dunn's second work of fiction. Her first, *Up the Junction*, was a series of stories or sketches, some of which appeared originally in the *New Statesman*, and in volume form in 1963. Both of these books had a *succès de scandale*, and were praised and attacked for their energy, candour and realism. Nell Dunn was hailed as an affiliated member of the non-existent school of Angry Young Men; she was seen to be writing of the lives of working-class women in a way that struck the same chords as the plays and novels of Sillitoe, Osborne and John Braine. Braine himself, writing of *Poor Cow* in *The People* declared 'I was disgusted, I was nauseated, I was saddened, but I was not bored', a comment which he may have generously hoped would sell copies: other critics offered more delicately formulated praise and attracted a more highbrow readership. I myself remember being struck in those early days not so much by the sensationalism of the subject matter as by the innocence of the emotions and the effortless elegance of the prose. But the books are sensational, and it is perhaps the combination of scandal and innocence that gives them their peculiar grace.

Nell Dunn did not set out to be scandalous. Her reports of life in South London are not 'worked up' or politically motivated: they are simple, apparently artless, sympathetic, participatory. And they are first hand. She herself moved to Battersea in 1959, made friends in the neighbourhood, and worked for a time in a local sweet factory wrapping liqueur chocolates for two shillings and sevenpence an hour. (Girls under seventeen were paid elevenpence an hour.) This was not her natural habitat; she was a refugee from smarter and more moneyed circles, but she got on well with her colleagues and they enjoyed listening to her written versions of their lives when she read them aloud. None of them seemed to think her stories were very shocking: life was like that, and here was someone who was telling tales they recognised. Nell Dunn was unhampered in her social and literary relations by any rigid formal educational conditioning: she had left school at fourteen and thereafter attended a variety of establishments at home and abroad. Like many adolescents, but perhaps in more extreme circumstances, she felt isolated, bored, cut off from the mainstream. Books were her company. She took refuge with Jane Austen and Sartre.

INTRODUCTION

Battersea was very different. It offered friendship, community, passion, warmth, instead of respectability and reserve. The openness, the quick responses, the lawlessness of the women she met there struck her as something new, invigorating, liberating. These were the early days of the new wave of Women's Liberation, and there, up the junction, Nell Dunn felt she had discovered a world where women did not depend on male patronage, where they went their own ways, sexually and financially, where there was plenty of work, so much work that they could afford to be cheeky, rebellious, loud-mouthed. If they lost one job, they got another. If they lost one man, they got another. The humour and the energy, the violence and the freedom were exciting. Nobody pretended, nobody was pretentious. It seemed a real world, where women could lead real lives. They did not seem oppressed, despite their low pay. There was a sense of matriarchy. Women were strong, openly strong, rather than deviously influential.

It is notoriously difficult to write across the class barrier without indulging in sentimentality or patronage. But Nell Dunn succeeds wonderfully, and never hits a wrong note. She does not moralise: her characters exist, freely, in their own world, without an ideology, without a superimposed interpretation. *Poor Cow* is a touching, truthful and fresh piece of work, written with an unselfconscious elegance that conceals its craft. And far from being saddening and nauseating, it has an exhilaration, a strange joy. Its heroine's name is Joy, and the choice is not wholly ironic, although she is also the poor cow of the title. When we meet her in the opening pages, she is walking down Fulham Broadway with a week-old baby in her arms, her 'slum-white legs' bare, wearing her maternity dress hitched up with her coat belt: her husband Tom has failed to collect her from hospital, and she's on her own with baby Jonny, as she remains through much of the narrative. But she is by no means a helpless victim: she is a survivor who admits to herself that she can't take too much security. This is just as well, as her life seems to be a catalogue of disasters, which follow naturally and inevitably from the first false step of letting herself get pregnant. 'What did I go and get landed with him for, I used to be a smart girl?' she asks herself on the first page, as she stares at her son. Her husband Tom has a lucky streak of thieving which translates her into a nice close-carpeted flat in Ruislip and when he's arrested Joy falls in love with Dave, an ex-colleague of Tom's, and they share a brief pastoral idyll. When Dave gets sent down too, Joy is left on her own again with little Jonny.

But she doesn't sit and mope: she works as a barmaid and as a model, goes out for evenings with her friend Beryl, exchanges views on life, men and prostitution with her Aunt Emm, tries to tempt her driving inspector and the untemptable solicitor Mr Pinker. She is amoral or immoral by the world's standards, but she has her own standards: she declines Beryl's suggestion of 'going up West to earn a bomb' in these terms: 'No, Beryl, I value my sex too much, it's all I've got; you lose the pleasure of it if you turn professional.' And the novel captures the pleasure of it, the fragility of joy, the helplessly persistent hopefulness of humanity, the self-renewing small pleasures of the flesh. The English novel has always tended to treat sex with reverence, prudery or titillation, and the woman's novel, until the 1960s and 70s, remained remarkably evasive and discreet. This was one of the first post-Chatterley books to speak out, to treat women's sexuality as though it were entirely natural, as natural as man's.

Technically, the novel is a *tour de force*. The narration is conducted on several levels, in several voices. The dialogue is rich and full of evocative one-liners, such as Auntie Emm's 'Me roll-on's gone a dodgy colour – I put it in the Bendix.' The narrator's voice is spare and cool: it describes, with a sparse elegiac poetry, the dereliction of London's back streets and suburbs, the comfort of pub and café, the cheap consumer attractions of the High Street. Joy's inner voice, in contrast, is intimate, colloquial, confiding, sentimental, aggressive and chirpy in turn; the author catches the living inconsequentiality of her thought processes without condescending to them – for Joy's fantasies of sex, domesticity and happiness are not subjected to authorial disapproval or satire. She is allowed her choices, her autonomy. We respect in her the logic of the illogical heart. Here is Joy, soliloquising:

> 'Then sometimes when he's home, he's good to me, that's another thing. If he were rotten all the time I could go but sometimes for a week at a time he's all over me. I can't do no wrong – I'm a smashing wife – he even lets me wear me pony tail – and I feel a proper mum, I feel great.
>
> Then, again, you read all this stuff in the papers – result of a broken home – delinquent locked up, all the rest. I don't want my Jonny to be the result of a broken home – if I could find a bloke tomorrow who loved Jonny as much as he loved me I'd go with him.'

This is authentic comedy, yet not at the expense of its subject. The joke is hers.

Joy's letters to Dave in prison also form a substantial part of the text and offer another, self-edited version of Joy's character. Resolutely cheerful, sexy and impressively ill-spelt, they mock many orthodoxies in a subtle and unobtrusive parody of romance and female expectation. Joy swears eternal loyalty, and sleeps with whoever takes her fancy.

> 'Well my love, I have something to tell you. ha ha. Me and Beryl have taken up Modeling ha ha Yes. Its alright

nothing bad we get £2 an *hour* mind you only 1 hour a week so far, I'll send you some photos in my bikeny Sexy ... Dave if my divorse come through I'll marry you straite away I promise you that.'

Sex, motherhood, cheap smart clothes, fun, domesticity: these are Joy's preoccupations. The descriptions of motherhood are particularly fine, and the treatment of the relationship between Joy and little Jonny is delicate, deeply sensual, and startlingly observed. There are sentences that evoke infancy with a stunning immediacy, and make one wonder how one could have forgotten, could ever forget. There have been so many novels dealing with maternity in the last twenty years that the subject matter no longer strikes one, as it then did, as new: but historically Nell Dunn was one of the first to notice such things – or perhaps one should say, to think them worth recording. We read of Joy working in the pub and remembering with a kind of physical rapture not only Jonny's small body but also his clothes: his tartan trousers with the hole in the knee, his Wellington boots, his best striped jumper, his Woolworth's drawers with blue dogs on. We read of them eating cornflakes in bed, and sucking spangles together. We read of Jonny's attachment to his small red battered tractor, which he won't go to bed without, which he won't relinquish even while Joy is dressing him: 'she pulled his red jumper over his head and he changed his tractor from hand to hand as she put his small arms down the sleeves'. The tenderness and the simplicity are lyrical: this is the real thing.

Joy is a good mother, a good, affectionate, demonstrative caring mother, although both her lover and her husband are in prison, although she makes love to other men both for sex and money. This distances her from a possible fictional prototype, the tart with a heart of gold, for this prototype (at least in the sentimental English version) is not usually equipped with a small child, or at least not with such a vividly presented, real, ordinary small child. The connection is arresting, slightly provocative. Nell Dunn's portrait reminds us that the sensuality of sex and the sensuality of motherhood are not distinct, separate, watertight compartments: they are intimately, naturally connected, they spring from a single bodily source.

I have sometimes wondered whether another myth or stereotype hovers behind Nell Dunn's first two works – the Orwellian myth of the emotional, warm-hearted, warm-blooded Working Class, superior both morally and physically to the mean-spirited, timid, reserved, petty Bourgeoisie. And there is, perhaps, a little idealisation here: not all working class communities are marked by warmth, spontaneity, and sexual tolerance. The working classes became fashionable, in the swinging sixties, and the faces that starred in the film versions of *Poor Cow* and *Up the Junction* were the faces of the sixties – Carol White,

Terence Stamp, Liz Fraser, Dennis Waterman. But Nell Dunn's work has a freshness, a firsthand observation, that is very different from its slick commercial copies, from the standardised versions of soap opera and sitcom. If there is a myth here, a myth of escape and liberation, it is a positive one, an enlarging one.

Much has changed since the sixties, and what was once considered 'raw' and 'shocking' is now perhaps more likely to be considered over-conciliatory, homophile, even sentimental by a later generation of feminist readers and writers. Joy is a poor cow, one can hear them saying, and serve her right if that's all she wanted from life: two shillings and sevenpence an hour in the chocolate factory, two pounds an hour posing in the nude, not much of a choice, when it comes down to it, they might say, she's selling herself cheap whatever she does. And her interest in men and sex would now be considered far from modish. One might well now view Joy not as a symbol of liberation, but as someone to be liberated. But Joy survives the tides of feminist politics and of sociology. She evades our disapproval. She is a survivor.

Margaret Drabble, London, 1987

POOR COW

She walked down Fulham Broadway past a shop hung about with cheap underwear, the week-old baby clutched in her arms, his face brick red against his new white bonnet.

She hurried along hoping she wouldn't meet anyone as Tom hadn't come to the hospital with her clothes, and she still wore her maternity dress hitched up with her coat belt.

Her slum-white legs were bare and her feet thin in the high suede shoes.

She went into a café, sat down and laid the tiny baby on the scratched-green bench beside her. She thought of what Tom had said when he first saw him. 'Why ain't the bleeder got curly hair?' The woman brought her a cup of tea. She had orangey-coloured hair, the crimson lipstick overlapping her lips. She walked with a slight limp in her open work sandals, with the black grease in the holes where the cream-coloured plastic rubbed against the bones of her feet. She carried a piece of bread in her water-swollen fingers, from the kitchen to the counter, and scraped a knife of marge across the top, then she took it back to the kitchen to put on a plate.

Joy felt starving hungry. She hadn't stopped feeling hungry since the child was born. The hot tea burnt her gullet, she felt it running down her throat.

The woman swept under the table with a yard brush.

Joy looked at her son. 'What did I go and get landed with him for, I used to be a smart girl?'

In the kitchen the wireless played:

I shan't be leavin' any more.

Outside in the street a young woman passed pushing a pram, a fag hanging from her lip. 'Now I look like that.' She ate the dark-brown cottage pie, mixing the mash in with her fork, a great relieving warmth filled her stomach and the sweet tea lifted her spirits. Above her head an ad with a lot of golden girls in bathing suits read COME ALIVE. YOU'RE IN THE PEPSI GENERATION!

'Fuck that,' she said as the snow fluttered thoughtlessly against the window pane. She put a penny in the Fortune Teller DON'T REGRET. TRY AGAIN.

Going up the road she met an old man with a dog and as the dog strained after her, the old man smiled and said 'In the spring a young man's fancy . . .'

Joy hurried painfully up the stone steps to her one-room flat. The whiff of sour lino hit her in the face as she opened the front door; it was odd slices of green-pitted lino she had sometimes seen saved by dustmen and tied to the back of their lorry.

Mrs Bevan hung over the banisters. 'A man broke in and done our meter last night. The police says "I pity you white women in this house with all these coloureds down the street." They could tell he was coloured from the finger prints.'

She went into her room where the embroidered flowers on the lace curtains twisted hopefully up the sunless window.

IN THE MONEY

Joy woke up one morning, the baby still latched to her breast. It was her twenty-second birthday. She put the kettle on to make some tea and looked in her purse. One and fourpence.

'I'm so skint I haven't even a pair of drawers to wear.'

She heard someone flying up the stairs and the door was flung open. She stood, barefoot, in her black nylon petticoat with the shredded bottom, her blonde-bleached hair sticking out from her head, Hottentot fashion. It was Tom.

'Happy birthday, sweetheart, we're in the money.'

He emptied a BOAC bag onto the bed and wads of dirty bank notes tumbled out. The baby screamed. The kettle whistled. Joy jumped up and down. 'How much – how much – who've you done?'

I've always been a daydreamer, me Joy – Joysy as my Auntie calls me. Daydreamed about – oh, loads of things – just to have something, to be something. I don't want to be down and out all the time I want – I don't know what I do fucking want but I dream about driving a car, that I'm in this big car driving around. When you've got a car you kind of feel something. It's a marvellous thing. I feel independent, let's put it that way. I feel like, well, it's mine. And I feel like pulling up at a bus stop and saying 'Do you want a lift?' Potty really, but I do. Oh and I daydream about the sort of house I'd like to live in. I know what sort of house I'd like. A house in the country. One of these old-fashioned houses. You know these old cottages, you remember the ever-so-old cottages, with little tiny windows, and I'll tell you what, they've got a long pathway and you know the trellis what goes over like that, that's the sort of house that I want. Ever so plain, I don't want nothing fancy, but just nice, like a proper little home. I'd have fitted wardrobes and I'd have all pale colours, I'd have blue and pink 'cause I like them. And I'd have a white dressing table, very very long, fit it in the windows. And I'd have just an ordinary bed and a white painted headboard. Oh yeah. Flash curtains I'd have. Coloured curtains I suppose, no, plain curtains. Oh, and a fitted carpet. Must be a pale colour, pale blue or something like that. Nice white bedspread. Look lovely. What would I do all day? Well first thing I'd get up in a morning to get little Jonny to school, then I'd do all my work and what would I do then? Let me think. Do me work and my washing and bleeding ironing. Then make meself up, and go out in me car. Shopping, go round my mates, then I'd come back and cook the dinner. I just like to feel that if I wanted something I could go out and buy it. Terrible when you ain't got fuck all, you ain't got nothing.

So we took a luxury flat out in Ruislip and furnished it out from the Shepherds Bush Market. We went down there in the Jaguar and bought a load of stuff.

Brought home a puppy, Rove I called it. The rotten poxy dog went and chewed up my new boots.

At first I liked it out there. I told the hairdressers opposite that Tom and Dave – Dave was Tom's mate he came to live with us – had their own business – well they did – thieving.

I used to push the pram around Ruislip. Little Jonny in his posh clothes fast asleep in the bottom.

Up the High Street past deck chairs, watering cans and cut-price jellies, past a notice announcing THE LILIAN FOSTER SCHOOL OF CREATIVE DANCE AND POISE. 'Special attention paid to Tone of Class and Deportment.' Past the war memorial and a wreath 'To dear old Stan and Nobby always remembered.'

I'd read all the notices 'A Chrysanthemum Show will be Held. Bunkers for Sale Cash or deferred terms.' And in a small shop 'Page Boy Attire for hire,' little kilts and sporrans and 'Mink stoles for hire.' Next door it said

'Inexpensive funerals,' I made a note of that for when I passed on 'cause I'm bound to be skint.

Joy walked on, over the common, where the leaves mingled with Smith's Crisps bags, iced lolly covers and sixpenny bus tickets.

'Once I pass me test and get me own car I'll be out all day whistling at the men.'

On the muddy grass a blue plastic comb and a sweet paper. She sat in the bus shelter and read the *Daily Mirror*. Next to her sat two smart women in white shoes.

'We did it all in waterproof concrete then we had it waterproof-rendered.'

'No I never speak to the man next door – I don't want to get involved.'

On the red brick church opposite, it said – IDLENESS IS THE ROOT OF ALL EVIL.

'When we just got married the world was our oyster and we chose Ruislip.'

A policeman came up and Joy gave him a smile.

'What you up to?' he said, looking in the pram.

'Watching the people,' said Joy. The policeman said, 'You should pay more attention to nature and not to wicked human beings, what you want to know about human beings for, they're all wicked.'

Across the way at the Civil Defence Office, Joy tried to join.

'Well, there are a few sections. The Men Only – we'll have to rule you out of that. Can you do First Aid? I could pick you up in one of our ambulances.'

'Oh yeah,' she said, 'my old man would kill yer.'

The sun shines on the pollarded trees and an old lady sits on a bench in a print dress, come down to see what's going on.

Rosebay willow-herb and lupins lean against the rabbit hutch. The house where the fourteen-year-old boy got into the bath with the two-bar electric fire on Christmas morning. And when his mother came to call 'Turkey's done', she found him shocked to death; and on the mirror in her lipstick she read 'I hate Ruislip'.

'When I lived at Clacton the road had a station at each end, and all day long I'd sit at the window and watch the people pass – but here you can sit and you won't see no one only the cars comes home of a night.

'All they do here is clean their places ... What's the point of worrying about a bit of dirt – you're well covered with it when yer dead and buried.

'I miss the ice-cream man. Hokey Pokey they used to call it. "Hokey Pokey penny a lump, the more you eat, the more you jump."

'Poor old dear she's a right nutcase. That's all there is here; either they won't speak to you at all or they're cranks.'

'I come from Stanwell. I was a barmaid there. It's a

raffish place really. There'd be parties down on the motor launches after closing time ... you never knew who you'd end up with ...'

'Oh they'd never stand for that sort of thing in Ruislip – too proper.'

Down an empty street the milkman comes slowly, in his red cart: DRINK A SPRINGTIME PINTA.

'Hey the chimney-sweep's bin in "Shangrila" all morning and she's only got one chimney.'

After her walk she'd go back to the close-carpeted flat, take Jonny out of the pram and lay him down on the floor, and herself down beside him, like she'd seen in the advertisements. He'd kick and smile and she'd bury her face in his stomach and make him laugh. While he was awake, and she was busy around him cooking him up tiny meals, ironing his playsuits and brushing his sparse black hair, she was all right, but when he fell asleep she was overcome with desolation. On cold days she'd warm his cold feet under her jumper pressing them against her bare stomach. He'd laugh and push his face up against hers so all she could see were his round eyes distorted by the closeness, and they'd both laugh.

TROUBLE

Sometimes Tom and Dave stayed out at nights, then we'd be all alone, me and little Jonny. It was winter then and very black outside, just a few sparse lights. He'd wake up screaming hungry in the middle of the night and I'd lift him from his hot, wet bed into mine. Straight away he'd latch his mouth onto my breast and, lying like this, one against the other – he'd be all damp. I liked the smell of his wet body, I half asleep, him sucking, and the rest of the world blacked out. Sometimes I went right off and woke up to find him asleep, mouth still buttoned onto me nipple – artful little beggar. I'd be frightened to wake him, and terrified less I suffocated him. We was company to one another when Tom was out all night, up to God knows what. Never marry a thief.

Sometimes little Jonny would go quite hysterical, scream and scream. I don't know if it was the wind or what and then I'd have to lie him, belly against mine, and rock him on my body till he'd go quiet, his wet mouth against my neck. I'd listen to his quiet breathing catching the faint smell of his breath. We got very close him and I that winter.

But Tom wanted good times. He always said that we'd have a great big car, I'd have diamond rings and everything else and when you haven't got it that's everything you want. He didn't really want to be happy, or be married like we was. He always wanted more out of life than what he had.

Well, sitting indoors I didn't know what was going on. I used to think, 'God somebody else might want him.' I thought it was marvellous because he was so exciting but then I'd walk down the street and see people together with their kids and think, now if he had an ordinary job he'd respect me more. But when you've got plenty of money you can buy anybody, I don't care who it is. You can buy them and you lose your respect for women.

But the flat, it was really beautiful. I'm not exaggerating, it really was a lovely flat. We'd spent all the money going in it, bought all new lino for it. We had everything. The bath felt like satin, yer arse just skated along it. I never knew one bath could be so different from another. Oh it weren't half lovely. And we were going to have a bar. We was planning how we was going to have it and then Dave came to live with us and Tom started to get nervy. He was getting on edge, and Ruislip was getting on me nerves. Sex is getting me down, it's making me repulsive about it –

Tom's got so old fashioned – he doesn't want to do this and he doesn't want to do that. When I want to feel sexy – I stand looking at myself in the mirror and hitch up one shoulder and stick out my breasts. He just wants to sit and watch TV when he's home.

One night I'd had a bath and I was lying in bed waiting for Tom to come up and I was wanting it so much, and then I hear him coming up the stairs, and by the time he come through the door – I didn't want it no more – I didn't want him to touch me.

Then one day, he'd just done a job – we had £900 in cash; it was just before Christmas. We was driving down the Bayswater Road in this ringed Mercedes and suddenly the law was after us, pulled us in and lifted the bonnet to see if the motor was ringed, and Tom just drove on – knocked two coppers flying and drove on – with the bonnet up. He couldn't see a thing. He turned up a one-way street, smashed into the wall, and we all jumped out. He dragged me and little Jonny out and pushed us in a cab.

Well the next day about five o'clock in the morning, the police come. Me and Tom was in bed and before we knew where we was they come to take him away. They done him for forty-two charges.

He got four years, course he only had to do two years, two years out of that you see. We'd spent all our money and then all of a sudden he was gone, just like that. Police come, took him away. It was a terrible shock. Ruislip doesn't sound far to you but to me it was a long way away, because I've never been out of Fulham or Chelsea. Oh it was a lovely flat. But I hadn't even the heart to sell the furniture, I just walked out and went to live with my Auntie Emm.

AUNTIE EMM'S

'I had a fight with this woman on the landing,' said Auntie Emm – 'she hit me with a broomstick and I hit her back. I'm sure she's stolen one of my plastic egg cups – it's a red one that's missing and I know she likes red – she's a nutcase really – she was in Banstead for two years. I always seem to have nutcases in the room next door to me.'

Joy was back in Fulham. She'd moved in with her Auntie Emm, who lived in one room, off National Assistance, and pills. Out of the window she read RUSSIANS ARE BEST and I LOVE MYSELF painted on the brick wall. Dog roses ran riot over the pigeon coop, and on the line a bellyful of colours flapped in the breeze.

Auntie Emm wore mock-crock shoes and a peek-a-boo black jumper without a bra. She rattled on while Joy sipped the gas-ring tea and held little Jonny on her lap.

'When I was fifteen I ran away to Paddington. Those

were the days. There's not much money in sex nowadays, too many people are doing it.'

'Oh yeah,' said Joy, trying not to get down-hearted.

A yellow plastic bucket stood in a tin basin on the floor and just above the bird cage with a cheeping, captive budgie.

'He was half a woman and half a man, mothadite they call these people – mothadites.

'He made me sweat and when I sweat I can't stop so I runs in the kitchen and I'm squirting that body mist all over me and he says, "What on earth are you doing?"

'He's a very clean fellow – I do admire a clean fellow.'

The sun shone in hot through the window onto the mauve candlewick bedspread. They were burning the grass in the graveyard. Men in blue dungarees leaned on rakes, dark against the sun; the spring had come.

'I hope you haven't got no bugs here, Auntie Emmy.'

''Course I ain't got no bugs, what do you take me for – bughouse?'

'I'm fed up with buggy places.'

Emm took her corset and stockings out from under the cushion on the armchair and pulled up her skirt. The veins were tangled on her shaky hands. 'I've been waiting all this time for me change of life so I can go on the town with no worries. I might even go further afield to seaside places and speculate it. I had a fellow called Blacky, he was one of the finest fellows going – he was nicking lead and all that. One day he bought me a bracelet from Woolworth's and I said "I don't want that, I don't like nothing like that dangling from my wrist – I like good stuff." You never know who you might team up with in one of them seaside places. I want someone with a good position that I can look up to and say, "Oh he's mine".'

Jonny had fallen asleep and Joy laid him on the bed wrapped in his pink blanket. 'I thought it was going to be a girl that's why I got a pink one. Do you know Auntie Emm, I'm beginning to wonder what I'm saving meself up for.

'Remember that party for my twenty-first birthday? Tom had just done a job. Seventy pounds worth of whisky we had, and the food, an army couldn't have eaten their way through it – most of it went bad the next day – it was a hot night, remember?

'I didn't love the baby when he was born. I hated him really for separating me from Tom. Then when he was nine weeks old we was in this poxy flat before we moved to Ruislip, he got chicken-pox with complications and the doctor said he would probably die. They took him to hospital and put him on the danger list – his whole body was raw with the spots, his little lips were just two scabs and he couldn't suck or swallow – he even had the spots inside his mouth and down his throat. He was getting weaker every day – it was only then when I thought he was going to die that I loved him. But when I came out of hospital in an old drape coat that had gone out of fashion – bolero maternity-dress, beige shoes and no stockings – I thought "Fuck me. Whatever did I go and do this for, a five minute wonder and it's all over".'

Auntie Emm pulled her stockings up over her veiny legs. 'Five minute wonder, but what a wonder. My mother had ten children in two rooms – my father was a drunkard – most men were then – and a lot of women too. There was nothing to do at home so they went to the pubs – there wasn't even any comfy chair just a kitchen table and sometimes one armchair. When there wasn't any money she went out and scrubbed doorsteps – if finally there wasn't any money they took your children away from you and put you in the workhouse.

'I was kicked around as a kid – and I vowed no matter what happened I'd take care my kids never got badly treated – I used to kneel down and pray at night "Dear God, don't let me die before my kids are old enough to fend for themselves." Now they're all grown up into fine kids and I don't care now what happens to me.'

Up in the bathroom notices hang: DO NOT WIPE HANDS ON CURTAINS. PLEASE CLEAN THE FLOOR AFTER USE OF BATH. THE LANDLORD.

Joy filled a bucket with water to heat for Jonny's nappies. Emm had turned the radio on and was bawling above the pulsating music.

What a day for a daydream,
What a day for a daydreaming boy.

'What do they know, they know nothing, they haven't even felt pain – men aren't capable of feeling pain like women. I'll use them if I feel like it but in the morning I'll tell them to move on. They use you to prop them up, they like you to think you need them to earn your bread and pay your rent but it's a big lie when you can perfectly well get it off the Assistance. I'm tired of pretending I love one of them – I used to pretend I loved and then directly I was crossed, down came a black curtain and I didn't love them any more.' Emmy combed out her red-rooted hair.

'I have lots of offers now but I am a bit nervous – being in the change. First I'm going to get myself put right then I'm going to go to town and it'll be all town.'

She stood in front of the mirror sticking on false eyelashes over her big bloodshot eyes.

'What sort of a life have I had? Go to work – come home and the old man grumbling at me. The one that's after me now, he's old but he's good, elderly men I've got a lot of faith in – I like 'em old – this one I've got now he's lovely – I keeping testing him, putting him through the test – you've got to put 'em through the test, find out if they do want you or not. I say "Do you love me? Don't ever leave me." Men come up to me and they ask me to go out with them and I size them up and down.'

AUNTIE EMM'S

The radio crackled on,

And I'm lost in a daydream,
Dreamin' 'bout my bundle of joy.

'This one he runs a fruit stall and he's going to put me in one – oh, it's lovely, it's beautiful.'

Joy got out the floor cloth and started to wipe over the lino while Auntie Emm rattled on.

'My happiness had gone – there was no happiness with Jack – he didn't want to go out, he wouldn't drink. He was always too tired to go out – he was seventy-four, too old. I stayed at home all that time waiting for the kids to grow up – then I wanted to come out a bit but Jack, if he saw me sitting by the tele knitting, he was as happy as the flowers in May. That sort of life makes yer nerves bad – I like to be out and about. I told this Len all my 'istory – he knows who I've been with. Once Jack caught me kissing this Len on the corner of the street – he called me all the prostitutes, called me an old cow and all that – I never spoke to him no more after that and six months later he left. Len was all for it, he was going to get me a flat and he was going to stay with me and all that – then he went the other way. He's afraid Jack's going to have him up for the money – divorce me and take him up the court. Nothing satisfied him – some women would never have stayed with him as long as I did and I've not had a happy life you know – he's had other women as well as me. He'd get me waiting outside the bloody cemetery gate for him hour after hour and never turn up.

'Then I got these two rooms in Reform Street – my sister was living with a flower-seller. Maggie fetches this flower-seller back – so of course we all go out and have a good drink and then thunder and lightning come up, and Jack's living at Wandsworth – so of course that was the start of the performance. She was over one side and I was over the other – well that was the night we both fell. Then she got me into debt with the tallyman and we had a fight in the middle of the night, right out in the road – she's been more gay than I have, she has.

'So there I was, he could see I'd been crying, and he pulled up in his motor and said "What's the matter?" "He doesn't want me," I said. "And nor don't I," he said. So I thought there's only one thing for me to do, go and drown meself out of the way. But I changed me mind later, and when I come back, bleeding cheek, he'd sold all me home to the second-hand shop. So I went round to this woman's house and I said, if you want him, you take the kids as well. I'd had two kids in the twelve months. And then, unexpectedly, on Kings Cross Station I gets off with a soldier. "Where do you live," he said. "I live at Fulham." "Well, I live at Islington, would you like to come home with me?" "Oh no," I say. When I get home he'd got another woman in cooking a chicken. "Upstairs you," I said. "You're not cooking no chicken in my kitchen – your place is upstairs, not down here." We'd had ructions for ages and one day I called him out the kitchen and said, "One of these days you'll be a bleeding old man and then I'll have a good time, don't you worry".'

Joy looked round for something else to do to take her mind off Auntie Emm's interminable and depressing chat.

'I was going to leave him to go in the Naafi – well you know how the war was. I started going out and having a good time – go out and have a drink in the pub and get off with a bloke and let him see you round the corner. I thought it was wonderful – you know that hairstyle when yer hair come up round the front in two swoops – we were standing at the mirror we were laughing me and my sister Jenny, trying out styles and I was standing with my feet in the water – I used to do me corns every Monday – and the air raid warden come up to say there was a chink of light – that was the start of that one – and he was a one and all.'

Joy wrung out the washed nappies and held them up to her face. She breathed in their faint warm smell and thought, 'somehow with Jonny I'll be all right – I I must, I must, I must . . .'

'You're far better off living with a man than married. When you're married there's no security. If you love one another he'll either leave you and come back to you – if you're married they know they can't get away from you. I've experienced both and believe me you're better off living with a man. I love men's company, I don't like women's company – a man will help you when a woman won't – you can go out with a man for a cup of tea – you talk to him – you tell him everything. They accept it, whereas a woman would say – Oh you shouldn't do that or I wouldn't do this – women are always trying to clamp down on things – frightened they are. Now the best thing for you Joysy is to find yerself a little job. I'll mind the baby – find a little cleaning job and get out and about.'

Joy leant out of the window to hang the nappies from a pole.

'That's all I've ever done – clean. I've bin cleaning since I was sixteen – I cleaned that tobacconist's shop for two years, remember? I cleaned the greengrocer's and the butcher's – I had to wear goloshes in the butcher's they give me a pair much too big and I slipped up and cut all me hand. I was only fifteen then when I worked in the butcher's. I've done some cleaning in my time. Blokes and cleaning, you'd think that's all there was in life. From the time I can remember my mum was always on about blokes, blokes, blokes that's all I've ever heard – well mums aren't like that.'

For some weeks Joy stayed with Auntie Emm. During the day she scrubbed the place from top to bottom, even washed the curtains twice, 'to try and make the place bright for Jonny's sake.' At night he lay beside her under the candlewick bedspread, Auntie Emmy snoring cheerfully after her six Barbiturin, washed down with Ovaltine, 'for Sound Sleep'.

Often Joy lay awake trying to fathom out the meaning of her existence.

I'd just like to be secure. You know, something out of life that everybody else's got. When I'm walking down the road I see people happy, I want that, but when I come to think of it I can have it one day and I may not want it. I'm not going to have much excitement once I settle down. At Ruislip I wasn't happy. I used to like to think I had a home and I used to like to think I had a husband to come and kiss me, you know, 'love', and all this sort of thing. It wasn't really like that, it was all false.

I wish I had a career. I need one more than anything. I regret getting married. In one sense I do, and in another sense I don't ... Let's face it, if I wasn't married I'd never have had all the excitement I've had ... Because I wouldn't have known what it was all about ... Then if I hadn't got married I'd have been an ordinary person in fact I might have been twice as worse as what I am now ... Wouldn't I really? A right old boot. I've always wanted, not power, but I've always wanted to have something that was mine. If I'd have been like an old brass I'd have had power. I'd have had everything I want and men, it don't matter who it is, what you're like, if you look a right old crab like Auntie Emm, let's look at it that way, I'd still have had it because men would have still fancied me. They wouldn't fancy me, they'd have fancied sex, wouldn't they?

And sex, it's killing me every day. If I don't have it, let's face it, I'm only human, I don't want to be all my life without it, I shall get very perverted in time to come, very perverted. I don't want to be left with nothing. I must have something. Little Jonny, I want him to have everything. I want someone who really loves me and loves little Jonny. There ain't such a thing though, men are so heartless.

LOVE

One day Dave came to see Joy. Dave had lived with them at Ruislip for a time and Joy had been fond of him. He was tall and wild looking and a bit of a crank, you never knew which way he was going to turn next. He had a hunted look in his big barmy eyes and had been in and out of Borstal all his life, but there was something about him that Joy liked. He understood about taking pills and getting blocked, and by this time Joy had sampled one or two of Auntie Emm's National Health quota. He understood about despair and clinging on and all the sort of wild feelings that Tom had never understood, being just a thick-headed thug.

Dave began to take Joy out. He'd bring a few extra pills for Auntie Emm, as a thank you for baby sitting, or sometimes they took Jonny as well. Dave would toss him right up in the air and Jonny would screech with pleasure but Joy would be on edge less he threw him right out the window. That's the sort of thing Dave would do and say after, 'I was only putting the poor little bleeder out of his misery.'

One day after Dave had cracked it for a few hundred he took Joy down Woolworth's and they bought up half the shop; plastic boats, windmills, turquoise shorts, mechanical robots, lamps with bowls filled with laminated fibreglass flowers, records with titles such as 'My Girl' and 'Wild Thing', and laughing they piled brown-paper bags on the back seat of the Jaguar and drove back to Dave's flat on the Chancellor Estate. Dave got it off his brother-in-law when he was nicked.

Then they got blocked. Joy lay beside Dave undoing his shirt, button by button…

There was this old record playing 'Stand By Me', how does it go? Kenny Lynch singing:

> *No I won't be afraid, I won't be afraid*
> *As long as you stand by me*
> *Darling, darling stand by me*
> *Oh-o-o-o Stand by me.*

Over the top of the bed was this plastic chandelier – and all the beams started falling like crystals, falling down on top of us, he was going so slow and I was coming so much…

*

LOVE

The next day Joy and Jonny moved in. Dave was only living in one of the two rooms. Joy took a look at the other. A battered, broken umbrella hung on the back of the door – old bacon rind and crushed food where the cooker once was. A gas mantle jutted from a cracked wall.

'You see, Dave, in a week it'll be perfect. I'll get little cottage curtains, wallpaper it out, it'll be just like a country cottage.'

So they went down the North End Road and bought a mural of a lake in Switzerland, topped by snowcapped mountains, and five rolls of left-over lilac wallpaper, for a pound, and triumphantly carried them home. On the way they stopped off at a furniture shop and put the deposit down on a bedroom suite, a brand new cot for Jonny and a shiny yellow kitchen cabinet. 'Deliver them tomorrow, please.'

That night Joy lay entangled in Dave's arms and thought, 'Even if it's only for six months that might be six months of happiness and anyway it's six months of life got through.'

In the mornings she'd do the cleaning while Dave put up shelves or painted the walls or made wooden trucks for Jonny. They'd tune in to Radio London. She'd sweep the floor; the dust rose and fell as the room gradually became tidy. The dishes washed and stacked, the mat rubbed over with the giant carpet sweeper. Dave would be hammering, his broad back under his pale blue T-shirt, his arms long and strong as he filled the kettle for a cup of tea. Hanging the clothes out on the line, strung across the iron balcony. The blue-cotton shirt – the one the colour of Dave's eyes – and Jonny's tartan trousers with the hole in the knee. Joy looked down into the grey well of dustbins below and wondered why anything ever had to change. Later in the morning they'd go up the launderette pushing the pram, a bundle of washing stuck on little Jonny's feet.

Sometimes he'd cook the dinner and sometimes she would, and after dinner all three would have a lay down.

'It's your turn to seduce me today,' says Joy, and very gently he took off her stockings. The room was warm and the curtains closed against the afternoon light and they lay on the bed, slowly and minutely examining each other's limbs. Later he made her a cup of tea and brought it to her in bed. The rain fell on the skylight, she was washed away by his body.

'I'll look after you,' he says, pressing her head against his chest. She felt the hair curling against her lips.

'If houses could tell secrets – no kidding – this house would have had more sex in it than any other house in London.'

If it were fine when Jonny woke up, they'd go to the park or a bit of a walk.

They were going along the street and she saw this great bunch of roses and tulips lying on the back seat. 'Get them for me Dave,' she said, and he was in there like a flash. He still had a hundred pounds in fivers in a Tetley tea-bag tin in the kitchen, so he didn't have to go out thieving.

The six o'clock sunlight was bathing the eggs and bacon as they ate their tea – the new budgie hanging just outside the window.

'There was this man down our road got cancer of the throat,' said Dave. 'So they operated on him and put him in a plastic voicebox – the first one they've ever done and then they taught him to speak – it comes out in a sort of screech you've got to be very quick to catch what he's saying. It's a sort of screech just like a budgie talking. That's what reminded me – him out there sounds just like him.'

'Oh Dave – the poor blighter.'

He held Jonny on his knee. He was a beautiful child, his hair, almost black and fine as silk, clung like feathers round his small white neck. His little limbs rounded and soft and his small legs sticking out of his nightshirt.

They made a cupboard, under the rafters, into a room for him. They painted it white and bought a white cot with a pink teddy-bear transfer and she built a shelf at the end of the cot so he could see five teddy-bears through the bars to keep him from desolation. His eyes were like blue pebbles.

Joy wondered how she could ever have thought herself in love with Tom now that she knew Dave. 'I can have sex with Dave every night and know that he don't want anyone else.' And indeed he didn't, he told her: 'I think about sex for about half an hour when I wake up in the morning then it passes then later on I think about it again going over the exact details of when I last seduced you, that takes me another two hours and then I might think about it for another hour or so in the afternoon. In all I think about sex for about four hours a day.'

When the weather seemed to have settled they went camping. They drove off, piled into the grey Jaguar with a tent, a cooking stove, a load of blankets and Jonny.

'I'd like to have a Rolls,' said Dave, 'but you know you have to go before a board before you can have a Rolls Royce – then they see if you're suitable – if they think you've got the means and that to run it ...'

They drove all day, stopping to buy maps and ice cream. They drove on till they came to Wales.

'I hope there aren't no insects where we stop. When I was a little girl my head was running with fleas. I could never get rid of them – then I went into hospital to have my tonsils out and when I came out of hospital I never saw another flea – that was the very last I saw of them.'

The car bumped and scraped up the gravel road; on the gate a notice said PRIVATE RIGHT OF WAY KEEP OUT. It was dry and rocky, only small bent trees and a ferny grass grew. At the crest of the road a waterfall spilt down the mountain, cascading under the road and splashing out underneath in a foaming spray over the rocks.

And then there was a great big waterfall, I don't know what the place was called, and it really was, oh it was fantastic. And all the water come from the mountain in a rushing cascade. It wasn't a dream, it really did. And we had it right on top of this waterfall. You know when you stand up there looking down, and you know the green there, the moss and the rocks, it was terrific, it was like a mad thing, little Jonny was sleeping under a tree.

The next night we goes into this big forest. So we gets in there and all of a sudden there's a great big hole and we goes down it. Oh it was fucking mad – in the Jaguar, and I kept laughing. We were going to put our tent up and I kept laughing so he said, 'Go on laugh,' he said – (this is Dave) – 'The suspension's gone.' I didn't know what the suspension was. I just stood there and rolled up. He said 'The suspension,' and I could see him getting mad, now I stop to think, he was getting mad. He said, 'I'll never get home, what are we going to do?' I was happy to stay here you know, I kept laughing. Anyway this farmer come and it was mad really. Dave's strong and he was trying to push it but he couldn't do it and yet this farmer come up and just got it out. And then we pitched the tent. Dave used to fill up the cans and hot the water up for us and Jonny had the first wash, I'd have the second and Dave'd have the third.

We'd walk for miles, Dave would carry Jonny on his shoulders, he was starting to say things like 'cow', 'moo-moo', 'woof-woof' – we'd walk along the three of us – daft really.

The only time we quarrelled was when we made a stew. And Jonny's one was too hot, you know, me giving in to Jonny and he'd put the stew there and I said to Dave you can't have that one, that's Jonny's, you know how you are, and with that Dave started over something. The stew had got hair in it, or Jonny was throwing grass, and he went fucking mad, so I said, 'There's the stew' – phum, and chucked it up in the air. I could do those sort of things with Dave but I couldn't do them with Tom. Many times I've been indoors with Dave and he's said something and I've chucked a cup of tea over him. Just for giggles.

One night we was camping on this farm and all of a sudden all the fucking cows come, frit the guts out of me. Didn't know what it was. It was pouring down with rain and he kept saying to me, 'Don't touch the tent cos the rain comes through'. Well I did and the rain did come through and all; we was saturated. So we had to go and dry all the things and then we walked. We went to Blackpool and we went into this fortune teller, cos I'm a bit superstitious and she give me a magic bean, she called it. Well it was an ordinary bean dried up, and we give her a shilling for it and she tells your fortune. And you sit there and she says 'The man you're with today,' and you was telling her, you know, you wanted her to tell you what you were saying, so you're just telling her what's happening. She said 'You're running away,' but I'd told her this. In my own way. Ridiculous, but we believed in it. She said you'll be with him in years to come. But it was mad because I didn't know who I was going to be with in years to fucking come. She didn't tell me if I was married, she told me I'd travel – I've fucking travelled nowhere. And I'd go in a big building, Gawd knows where that is. The only big building I've bin in is the Old Bailey.

We went to loads of places, then ten days after we come back well that was terrible. We come back, Auntie Emm had kept all the flat lovely. I used to send her money home, you know, couple of bob, if it's only ten bob, cos that's a lot you know, to Auntie Emm, cos she's on National Assistance, anything's all right for her.

Dave bought me some fantastic curtains. They were green and silver striped, all lined. Dark green and silver. Oh they weren't half lovely. Didn't half used to look lovely in that little flat. I used to have a long thing coming out of there with a big bamboo shoot and on there was all the shells what we'd collected and I used to lacquer them with varnish. And put the names on, Cromer, Aberystwyth, Pontypool. We went to Norfolk yes, didn't half do some miles we did. And we wrote with ordinary Biro, on the stones. And I stuck them along the shelf. And he made my shell up on the side, you know, a coconut shell. He used to get pictures, and he stuck them in the ashtrays. It was potty, but it was nice – it's things you never forget.

Back home again, the curtains closed, Jonny asleep and Radio London full on, Joy cooked a large steak-tea, done for about ten minutes each side, fat chips and cabbage. They lay on the bed, a tap dripping out on the iron balcony, having a second cup.

'You look like a sex kitten when you put your arm over your face like that Joysy. What about us going in for a baby? Company for Jonny. I'll buy you a new maternity dress every week, even if I've only got thirty bob.'

Outside the window someone shouting. 'You're a cunt, a cunt,' ripping the gentle night.

They looked out across the yard. A little bloke shouts, 'You dirty cunt,' and rips the vest off the giant bodybuilder and the body-builder stands naked to the waist in the road while people drifting out of a party in low cut dresses and fancy hair-dos stand and watch.

Joy lay down again. 'Which part of me do you like best?'

'Your toes – that's the only part I reckon,' and gently he took off her blouse and gave her love bites down her stomach.

And Joy thought of the window in the high street full of tiny frilly dresses, almond-pink with panties to match and the toy babies with smiling rosebud mouths, and she hoped for a girl.

The next day was a dark thundery day full of storm, and

rain making everything shine – the glass roof and the pink lino, discarded on the balcony. In the distance the trains flew by all lit up as though it were night instead of four o'clock in the afternoon.

Joy stood in the kitchen in her petticoat, bare-legged, her hair down her back, ironing her new blue skirt. On the draining board were the plates unwashed from toad-in-the-hole, the tea cups scattered, and Jonny asleep on the settee, his bottle still half full of tea in his mouth, his cheeks slightly flushed. And just nearby the wooden drying rack decked out with underwear. 'I like to have my smart drawers round me.'

Dave was in the bedroom practising his guitar – he rather fancied himself as a pop-singer.

*I'm justa wander boy I go where nature
feels she wants to guide me . . .*

She liked standing in her tight petticoat and bra in the warm kitchen. She liked the feel of her hair on her bare back. The evening sun came through the skylight and lit up the turkey mat.

Dave played on:

And I'll do my living as it comes along . . .

Their life together was a series of treats. When they woke in the mornings he'd make a cup of tea and bring it to her in bed – if Jonny was awake he'd have some too, tucked in beside her, under her arm, laughing. Dave would read down the paper for a horse to back. 'I'll have a shilling on these three,' says Joy. 'Precious Pearl because it reminds me of meself. Flying High because that's you, and Mother's Day for little Jonny.'

Jonny was walking now. His face and hands and knees were always filthy, so Joy had to change his clothes three or four times a day. She loved doing this, holding his small warm body on her lap, pulling the T-shirt over his head 'pee boo Mama', he'd shout and fall back in laughter. She couldn't get over his lovely legs and little square feet. She let his dark hair grow long and thick so it curled in great feathers around his ears. She would sit for a long time looking at him as he played around the room or crawled out onto the balcony.

Dave was planning a big jewel robbery. His mates came nearly every day and they went into the other room to discuss details. It was planned for a few nights later. Joy's dreams had swept her into a rosy future. They would buy a shop, sell antiques. She would wear sloppy jumpers and buy a false pony tail from Shepherds Bush Market, hanging over one shoulder, but perhaps it had better not be from Shepherds Bush – a mate of hers had bought one and when she got home she found it was full of nits.

The planned night came. Joy got out the tin bath – 'You might as well be clean to go into a posh house' – and filled it with buckets of boiling water. Then she got undressed, 'Come on Dave, get in.' She sat at the back and he sat between her legs and soaped her feet for her, rubbing the soap on his hands and then between her toes, making her giggle. 'Remember Dave, I'd like some big thick sovereigns right round me hair – I'd look really gipsyfied, kiss curls. You should see my mate Sylvie who I worked in the chemist's with. I've seen some formy girls in my time but Sylvie beats them, she's tall, terrific tits, makes me look like a rasher of bacon beside her.'

Joy was in bed when Dave came home late that night, his pockets full of necklaces. He dropped them onto the eiderdown and climbed in beside her. She was asleep but she opened her arms and said, 'How d'you get on?'

'About a hundred thousand pounds worth between us – tomorrow we'll get rid of it. The old girl wasn't away after all – we had to lock her in the toilet but I let her out and give her a glass of water when we finished.'

When the police came for him he tried to climb out of the window – the Flying Squad was hammering on the door.

'Don't leave me Dave,' she screamed. So he came back and let them in, then they took him away.

MORE TROUBLE

They took him to Brixton on remand and Joy went to see him nearly every morning. Joy, young, skinny – skinny legs in the very high shoes that always looked one size too big – her ragged, bleached hair and the three guinea pony-tail she had bought from Shepherds Bush Market, to cheer herself up, pinned sideways up over her ear – a sandier shade of blonde.

And at night she wrote him letters. 'I'm lost, completely lost, we need each other so much and we can't have each other yet you're only a few miles away from me it's just not possible is it.'

And on the days when she felt stronger, 'Remember there's a future'; and 'Are you still cleaning your teeth and rubbing your shoes up? Black mark if you're not. Oh Dave I love you so much even though we're apart somehow you're near me like you say in our hearts I won't give up never. One day it will all be over.'

And at the bottom was a pink lipstick print of her cupid's bow lips. And, 'This must never beat us we won't let it because there is such a thing as LOVE'. And, 'I'm playing our records "Stand By Me" remember us playing it over and over again laying on the studio couch (Block) I just felt a shiver run down my spine (must have a think s ...). Oh the times I used to sing it – our memories will drive me mad.'

Enclosed in this letter was a half sucked bullseye.

'I can't seem to face things today.'

Then Joy got a job just down the road in the pub. It was the White Horse, a big modern pub with a lot of well-to-do customers.

They put her in the public bar to start with. She got a new black dress with see-through sleeves – spent the last of Dave's money on it.

There was a free room going at Auntie Emm's, so she left the Chancellor Estate and moved back there. Auntie Emm looked after Jonny during opening hours. She couldn't get to see Dave quite so often. His case was coming up soon but she still wrote every day.

'I told you this morning *I could not bear anybody else touching me. Oh Dave do you realise what you done to me.* I'm shore you made that Chanderler night for a perpers. I can wait for another 20 years for a night like that – I don't mean that BAD. I love You always and as days go by I'll love you more and more ... and make you feel the way you make me fill when you say the things you do. I feel so *wanted* and its a lovely filling. I'm not realy *brave* but I have so much faith that it will all work out for the best. Remember me always falling asleep? Oh God I'll never forget the Water Fall in WALES it was terrific.'

And another letter was stained with spilt perfume and she wrote, 'Oh don't it smell.' Dave wrote in red pencil in the corner, 'It smells of YOU (wonderful xxx)'.

And at the bottom of another letter she had put a row of stars – her special sign to mean love-making, and by the side had written 'please don't forget them.' And Dave added in his red pencil, 'How can I.'

At the top of Joy's last letter Dave wrote 'Please God give Joysy some peace now, please don't you see she can't take much more. Hasn't she gone through enough ... What do you want – our lives ... Well you're going to lose because our love will win, you hear we'll win so B————s to you.'

The day before his case came up Joy went up to see him, but he hardly spoke. That night she wrote: 'Oh love to see you unhappy makes me feel so sad, darling I love you so much, and I always will. Dave you think I'm going to let you down if you go away for a long time (I know you think that in your mind although you don't say it). Dave I won't let you down *Never*. Please believe me I love you and only you. Yes I know we have got a lot to face without each other. But if it realy was without each other we could never face it, so Always remember no matter where you are, I'll be with you, I know you can't see lovely things the Park, the Sea, but darling one day you will, I can't take Jonny over the park or to the fare because I feel the same way as you do. Although I'm out here it hurts me too. Darling you could have all my courage, but I would die without it.'

Joy took the next day off and went to the Old Bailey once again. Dave was being tried for robbery with violence. His mate had hit the old woman over the head and she had gone almost totally blind as a result.

She went by train and saw the lupins in the circular beds at Fulham Broadway and remembered the yellow gorse on the common near Pontypridd.

They let her go down into the cells to see Dave and they clung together. 'The first kiss since you was took, oh Dave.'

He was found guilty and the judge gave him twelve years. For a moment they looked at one another and then Joy, drunk, numb, faint, stumbling, staggered out into the air and leant against the wall of the Old Bailey.

When she got home she wrote to Dave: 'Oh Love today I was so shocked it seemed like the end of the world. I've cryed so much I can't cry no more. 12 years is sertaley a Long time. But it's not the end Dave. Please love try and face it. Your be by yourself for a long time. But I'll be out here waiting for you. I told you before no matter what happens I won't change I still Love you very much and *were still get married* one day. Dave don't give up love it's over now we no where we stand. I won't give up waiting because I want that family and happiness and most of all some one who loves me. Life hasn't finished for us it beginning now. Please try to face things. *I Love You Dave* more than anythink. Oh God so much I love you. You do believe me Dave don't you I will wait for you Dave. 12 years if I have to. How much you fill at this present moment? the same as I do. Lost and lonely but remmber our MEMORIES.'

And at the bottom Dave wrote, 'FIRST LETTER FROM JOYSY AFTER SENTENCE 12 YEARS OH GOD.'

That night she took little Jonny into bed for company and slept close against his warm, pee'd body.

Joy became good friends with Beryl, the Saloon barmaid. She was a big girl with tattoos all up her arms, 'Dad is best', 'Daddy's girl' and 'True Love'.

From opening till closing time she talked about men.

'The thing about him is he can dominate me – he's the only man I've ever met who can do that – he's a cigarette rep – he's very self-assured, he can make me do what he wants.' She bends giggling to collect glasses, her breasts in the low-cut black dress shake, round and high.

'I was a maid to this prostitute for eighteen months. I used to have to answer the phone. A bloke would ring up and say, "I want details of your personal service. Do you do whipping," and I'd say, "Yes," and he'd say, "What type of underclothes do you wear?" and I'd say, "Well, apricot and black" and he'd say "What do you look like?" and I'd say, "Long auburn hair and blue eyes," and he'd say, "That's nice, thank you very much," and slam the phone down or I'd say, "Now hurry up Sir and run round, you've got me all worked up with your questions."

'Some of them I pinch for myself if they want the harmless kinky stuff – I say to meself I might as well have the two quid as well as her – so I gives them this address. I mean I wouldn't go on the game meself – I don't mind them beating you with a couple of plastic roses (I don't tell 'em where I get 'em – off the Daz packet), and they're round my place like greased lightning – then I'll take me clothes off, sit on a bloke's knee and we'll have a little joke. "I like your titties." "Yes they are rather sweet" I'll say.'

Beryl had an enormous red-rimmed mouth and auburn hair caught back in a thick bunch. She wore a short black frock and her big legs bulged down towards her shoes. She always allowed the lace edging on her petticoat to show beneath her dress, there was something strangely dainty about her, in spite of her bigness she had small ankles.

'If you ever have any blokes, don't let them have it for nothing. You must charge 'em. I know you, you're soft. You must say "Here, I'm a bit hard up", or something like that, or "Could you let me have a few bob." You've got to get something out of them or they'll just use you – just use yer body – then go back to their wives and children.'

Joy listened faintly excited by the lewd talk. In the pub they called her Sunshine. One dinner time she had thirteen lagers bought for her. She only drank four, but with just a cheese roll in her stomach she was well away. Beryl rushed off in a hurry and Joy was left to help the guv'nor lock up. He was a major in the army, and said he was the Queen's first chauffeur – always drove the Queen everywhere. Then he got the job of manager at the pub.

'He's a dirty git on the quiet – his wife had gone to the hairdresser's and three o'clock closing time he locked the door and shoved me into his office, and said he fancied me. "I'm not like that." Said he'd give me two quid. "I'm not an old woman of forty yer know". "Well give me a wank then," he says. Well I hardly had to touch him and he wants it again next week and that's two quid extra on me wages every week; he was a major in the army so he is clean. I know at least he's clean.'

On the way home Joy bought a new suit for Jonny and a potted geranium for Auntie Emm. She couldn't wait to get back. She hurried along the pavement and ran up the stone steps through the battered, green front door and up the stairs.

'Auntie Emm, Jonny. It's Mama and I'm starvin'.' The child was lying kicking on the bed and she kissed him and buried her face in his stomach while he shrieked with laughter, then when she stopped he said, 'Bit more please Mama.'

The rent was up in No. 8, the flat she had shared with Dave, and one afternoon after closing she went to clear out the rest of her stuff.

She climbed the concrete stairs, her feet were heavy with misery. She unlocked the door into the flat and went in. It blew shut behind her – she hadn't been back since the day they took him away but the place had lost its loving feeling. She started opening cupboards and drawers and emptying out things on the floor to be sorted. A pile to throw away, a pile for Dave's mum, and a pile to take to Auntie Emm. She changed into her pink slippers and put an apron, tiny mauve violets creeping up in rows, over the top of her battered miniskirt.

Soon she was surrounded by her possessions. A plastic handbag without a handle, an orange deckchair, and a pile of shrunken jumpers and torn petticoats, which had had their day; Christmas lights, frosted glass candles in yellow and green and purple lay among them. And she remembered.

I used to run out to the toilet because our toilet was on the balcony and I'd have nothing on 'cos it was summer and he'd lock me out there. And he said, 'I'm going to drill a hole in that,' because I was always self-conscious about going to the toilet, and he said 'I'm going to drill a hole in there,' and I really convinced myself that he was going to drill a hole in the toilet while I was sitting on it. He was mad. A pair of sheets, a pink towel, a battered kitchen cabinet, a brown suit I conned off the WVS. Fuck me, what a load of junk. Me black dress with the flying panels, I couldn't part with it. Don't ever buy another one of these – a greying bra – it's one of them living things – don't give you no tits at all.

Then she sat down and wrote to Dave. 'Well my love, sorry about not coming up to see you this after-noon, I am now sitting in No. 8 writing this letter. God I have never felt so lonely in all my life. With 2 chairs and our coffy table (Joe's One). I am waiting for Joe (if he can make it) and also a man is going to buy our cooker I hope. Dave I'm alone. Now I will think of all our happy times. Remember when I used to call you up at the window, and wave all the kids are just going back to school. Oh I'm so lonely. Remember the night we put the curtains up – there gone now and our shelf with all the flower pots (Cakteses) and me always nocking them down and not forgetting Ceaser as well – Oh Dave its the end of our little home – No No No it can't be true. Oh Dave I'm so choked tears are running down my face help me Dave I need you so much and love you. We need each other so much. Should I give No. 8 up? Without you here it would never of been the same –

Wold it Love – *I Love You Dave*. I musent think its the end its the beginning we'll have another home wont we one day. This is the only pice of writing papper I have, so at least your have something from 8 wont you (even if its a bite of paper). I found the truck you made for Jonny (I'm going to keep it) I wish they would hurry up and come, so I could talk to some one but I musent forget you your by yourself all the time. "Selfish Joy" Not really A. xxxxxx We dont realise what we've got in each other is so wonderful people dont think it excises (But it does) We got a LOVE no one else got and it terrific its sending me mad. I'm so raped up in Your love I never wont to be un raped and I want to stay like it for ever I Love You – Dave I do. You should see all the dirt in the flat, Oh musent forget the rubbish ha ha. Your a cheat getting out of it. Remmber all the bottle and the 3 boxes of rubbish you was going mad with all the junk. (Thats Your Joy) Junk collector.

'They never did come and do the TV did they. Remmber creeping up the stair and looking left and right Oh we were mad. Hope I can find an envolock? Ten to one I cant. Not forgetting that night I went out and Auntie Emm caned your ear. ha ha. (Its on you Joy) We could never get rid of her when we wonted to the night we had the party and you went with them and I kept crying thought you had left me then you came back and cuddle me said you loved me. And you'd never leave me. Oh do you remember Dave It makes me fill Oh I dont know. By the end of the week it will be all gone. Then all we have is each other. But thats the mane thing *us*. Darling I be closing now must have a wash for the last time in 8 – And remember no one took Your place at 8 (that not ment bad) You under-stand what I mean.'

Underneath Dave wrote, 'From No 8 Our home now gone for ever.'

In the White Horse Joy began to ripen and blossom with her success. The regular customers all knew her and confided in her.

'She sometimes comes in at two or three in the morning, my wife.'

'Well she's probably just been at a party.'

'Don't give me that.'

'But don't you mind?'

'No, why should I? It makes it more interesting—'

'Aren't you jealous?'

'No, I had all that burnt out of me when I was seventeen. I was with this girl Doris who was a nympho and I was in love with her. She was it – she was everything and she just slept with anyone she fancied, she didn't even bother to lie – brother no one could go through that and come out the other end still jealous. No one.'

And Beryl's exuding, ripe body and continual stories: 'One was the waiter, one was a cocktail mixer. The cocktail mixer asked me to come back to his room. He said "Take your top off." I said "Who me?" He thought he was going to have the other.'

Beryl leant on the beer tap, her face lit up with the telling.

'I took me top off and he got right undressed. I've been out with some blokes but they've never got undressed altogether. When he was coming he grabbed hold of me really rough and I had me result. He was the cocktail mixer. He weren't half hairy and I love hairy men.'

And Beryl was full of wisdom.

'The trouble is people get married and their interests narrow and their minds deteriorate. They come home from work tired. They struggle for money and are pleased about the new telly and a good meal ...

'I reckon some people just aren't born respectable – I just never seem to have bin respectable. Though there was one bloke wanted to marry me. He was going up to Nottingham on a job. "I'm going to miss you love," he says to me all 'eartbroken. "Yeah," I says, "from what I hear there's ten women to every man up North so you should be all right." That was the last I saw of him.'

Joy still wrote every week to Dave.

'By the WAY my little Love have you been keeping your promises No dog ends on the floor? Have You? Also Jonny's got a terripine (its like a tortose) but he lives in the water, his names Bill, Jonny called him that, he loves him, I'll be glad when next year comes … I musnt spoil my letter by going all to pot, so darling heres a big kiss and I Love You and fancy you something terrible ha ha. Hold on, I'm just going to make a cup of tea. Auntie Emm driving me mad as usul. Oh by the way I know everything in barmaiding now ha getting good, A. Oh Dave, my feet ache through standing, I cant get Varicose veins can I, Oh I'd die. Oh there terrible Dave.'

One day she went up to the solicitor to see about her divorce.

'Have you ever committed an indiscretion Mrs Steadman?'

'Oh I don't know about that, what does that mean?'

'Had intercourse?'

'Only on one occasion and that was through frustration.'

'Only on one occasion?'

'Yes, I'm not that way inclined.'

She laughed at him and hitched up her bra but it appeared he wasn't that way inclined either. I would like a man with position, she thought.

On the day that Petal came into the pub Beryl was indulging in words of wisdom.

'I've bin a convenience far too long – now it's their turn to be a convenience.'

At the time Petal was working on bread delivery. He had big eyes and he walked with a swagger. There was a tear in the sleeve of his shirt and Joy wanted to put her finger through and touch his flesh.

First time he saw me he come right up to me and says 'Hello Blondie – What you doing tonight, Mouche?'

'Don't call me Mouche,' I said. 'My name's Joy.' Well I went out with him that night and I wore my brown suit – there's a load of buttons on it so you can't get out of it in a hurry and I had me hair all done up in a beehive. Well, he tried to put his hand up my skirt and I said 'I'm not like that you know.' Well that blew over and soon I was having it with him regular. He'd come round to my house seven-thirty in the morning when Auntie Emm and Jonny were still asleep – he'd bring me hot bread rolls straight out of the van – I let him have the key – and he'd bring them up to me in bed, make me a cup of tea and all. Cor he could put some down. But he was a bit deep that was the trouble with him. I never even knew if he was married. He was so soft I've never met a bloke like it, his hands were all warm and soft – it was the way he touched me. His fingers lit me up – I was all lit up. Next day he'd swagger into the pub, dinner time and say 'What'll you have Blondie?'

And what with the men, and the drinks bought her and Beryl, who was on about her friend Cherry who was on the game – 'She can't earn nothing in London it's too hot so she's gone down to Folkstone' – the world of the pub would close over her, the men laughing, and the smell of smoke.

Fat Mr Carter, a sanitary disposal engineer, coughing a mixture of beer and whisky, his jowls wide. 'Everything is graft in the building trade, from the sewers to the topping out. If I get a deal for a thousand pounds I get a hundred of that.' He buckled up with his loud laughter. 'The building trade is the foundation of progress but the labourers – you're dealing with a lower form of life.'

He looked around the saloon bar. 'All these men are very important people, very moneyed people – they're all big noises down here.'

And sometimes Joy's heart would sink.

Back at home she wrote to Dave.

'Dave, I'm not so blonde, I'm nearly back to my own colour, more Red. I'm going all plain and serfictcated ha ha go on laugh. And dont keep saying about that iffiey night, there shore to be many more you rotten sod. Dont forget on our visit to have your shoes polished and tie on. I'll have my eye lashes on. Sexy xxxx ... I've gone from one thing to another still that me. Did I tell you in September I'm going evening classes. Your never guess what for? Aleycustion lesson, how to walk propelye and some other thing anyway its sounds mad, but it will do me good. Oh Dave I going to realy try, your see my letters will sound right, and I'll talk all possh ha ha.'

*

Before she went to the pub in the evening Joy would bath Jonny in the kitchen sink. First she'd hang the towel out near the electric fire to warm. Then she'd boil up a bucket of water on the stove on the landing. When everything was ready she'd undress him. Peel off his jumper and knitted vest then lay him back on the bed while she pulled off his often damp trousers and pants. If she kissed one of his feet he'd hold up the other for her to kiss. As she soaped him all over with the flannel he'd fill his mouth with water and spit it out in a fierce jet and when she washed his hair he'd lie back his eyes narrowed up, his legs in the air submerging his head and spitting out water like a whale.

When later, she'd put him to bed and hurried off to the White Horse, it wasn't only his small body, but his belongings that she thought about a lot of the time. His tartan trousers with the hole in the knee she had bought in the North End Road last Christmas – everyone had been hurrying, buying smart clothes for their children to wear on Christmas Day to show off to the relations – there had been a kind of excitement, and even the stall holders had shouted with an extra gusto. Now these trousers were too small, they came just below the knee, but it didn't show when he wore his Wellington boots. 'Me boots, where's me boots Mum,' he used to say, almost sing; 'me boots, me boots'. His boots meant out of doors and down the road, small hand clasping tight a bar of chocolate, and the hopes of a plastic car or a balloon if he caused enough trouble.

Then there were his pants. She thought about his little cotton-knit drawers, two-and-eleven in Woolworth's with blue dogs running riot all over them. And his best jumper – she had bought it in a jumble sale on Clapham Common. It was burgundy-and-pink stripes, with short sleeves, and his little white neck stuck like a stalk out of the top, his black hair hanging in silky scoops over the back. She thought about this and about how he woke her in the morning, putting his face very close to hers and saying, 'Mum, Mum, I wanna see Mama.' And then, if she tried to go on sleeping, tried desperately to cling to the world of warm dreams, he would climb on her head, sit down and bounce about, or gently touch each eye and say, 'Mum open eye', putting his small mouth and often runny nose close against hers. Till finally she opened the covers and dragged him in with her and held him tight up against her, warming his cold feet between her legs. And then she felt an overpowering love for him – a love which didn't seem to have a beginning or an end. They would spit Spangles into each other's mouths as they lay in bed in the mornings, listening to the small throbbing transistor:

Here I stand, head in hand, turn my face to the wall
If she's gone, I can't go on, feeling two-foot tall.

He did quite a bit of singing himself – 'Baa Baa fat sheep' – he opened his mouth very wide and she could see his red tonsils dancing about in his throat and then he laughed a great hoarse, hearty laugh.

He could talk quite a lot now, he put his face very close to hers and spoke senseless words to her with the kind of intonations he'd heard others use. She would talk back to him about the animals he would get to know and the magic world, but many words he learnt quickly and would touch part of her body and say, 'Mama's leg, Mama's tum, Mama's bosom,' giving it a long slow prod with the tip of his finger.

Once he fell asleep on her lap in a bus and his cheek became printed like wallpaper with the creases of her blouse. And she, when she wasn't with him, still felt the imprint of his limbs against her.

TURNED ON

Joy wrote to Dave :
 'I think you may think, I'm just saying this because your away (I'm going to shout this bit.) WELL I'M NOT. I DO LOVE YOU AND IM GOING TO WAIT. AND WERE GOING GET MARRIED. (Hope I didn't deafen you) I love you **xxxx** Do you remmber when we went to that pub and they asked me to SING Oh it was terrible you made me go all RED, Dave you've had it now, your deffently dew now. Whats your punishments????? Dave were both make it up to each other one day, and I'll be a good *wife* too proper MUM. I love You so much. Dont worrie love I wont ever let you down NEVER. Without you and YOUR LOVE I be lost you dont know how true that is Dave. Oh darling I'm thinking of all what we taked aboat and I'll never regret what we done in Sex. We done so many wonderful things, and it wasnt wronge because we were in LOVE. Glad you liked the blouse, I brought it for you (you used to say why dont

you were blouses but I never liked them) I do now. I've nearly finished the kitchen it looks GOOD ha ha it should do as Randy Joy noes her job.

'Tomorrow I'll be going to Folkestone for the day. Oh I miss you even more then. Oh Dave I dont want to go with out you, Oh GOD why us why. I beging to fill chocked, but I musent I musent. Still Jonny will like it wont he? xxxxxx I dont suppose I'll wear the bikin? How was the sweets?'

And from Folkestone she wrote :

'Well love I'm sitting on the beach liserning to the Wireless (the one from home) radio Caroline. Auntie Emm's gone down by the sea with Jonny, Dad's eating a sandwitch (with no teeth in). Its nice and sunny very cold wind, so no bikin, I'm well raped up, wishe you were hear theres no sand only pebbels. Oh Dave Remmber when I bent down and you slaped my bum with that stick. Oh did it hurt. What was we doing. (Oh it was the wet sea weed and I had a stick writing things in the sand (Did it hurt) you loved it.'

The next evening she hurried down the road to the pub. It was raining, the smell of bacon drifted out of a café into the wet street. She was thinking, It's the summer – I get lonely in the summer, everything drifts out of doors really I like the winter – I like lighting the lamp and making tea.

In the bar Beryl was polishing the beer taps.

'I'm fed up Joy, I'm thinking of going up West again if

this modelling falls through – why don't you come up West? We could earn a bomb.'

Joy hitched up her bra. 'No, Beryl, I value my sex too much, it's all I've got; you lose the pleasure of it if you turn professional. Here, I've fixed meself up to pass me driving test – a bloke who comes in here knows one of the testers somewhere – he's going to give me my certificate if I have it off with him.'

'You going to?'

'Well I've got to haven't I – I bet he'll be a shrivelled up old crab of seventy – I'll just have to close me eyes – you'd do it for yer test?'

''Course I would.'

Joy was enjoying the pub, the men all liked her, and there was Beryl.

'I only once went on a blind date and then he turned out to be a Persian from Battersea. I can't go out with a woman I must have a man's company.'

'Every bloke I've been with has bin very, very clean that's my main interest – if someone doesn't look clean I won't have anything to do with him – well I'll give him a wank, I'm not that selfish.'

Beryl's arse big in her tight dress, handing out beer and quips to the men.

'He wrote me a letter, "Next time you come up the prison don't wear no underclothes".'

It was a lovely June day – Derby day – and everyone

was full of jokes, flashing five-shilling each-ways and writing out bets on the backs of paper bags.

'Coming with me to the Derby, me ole cock sparrow?' He leant across the bar to Joy.

'We'll know where you both are if we miss you,' says Beryl.

There was something about him she fancied – that's how it started, when she asked him could she have a drive of his car ... He was a butcher, he was all dressed up and yet you could still catch the smell of raw meat about him. He talked meat.

'A couple of pork chops I'd be sending her down every day, or a nice lump of steak – you've got to eat well, yer stomach is yer engine.'

That night after closing time Joy went home with him.

'Do you mind if I take me eyelashes off now we're indoors. Two-and-eleven, good aren't they?'

He had a lovely body – thick set – his legs must have measured sixteen inches round the calf and he had great big hands, red like raw meat, with big thick fingers.

Then there was the young sailor in the tight cotton suit lolling against the bar – he had black hair like her Jonny's and a thin neck. Joy was the first bird he'd ever had.

In the afternoon she sat at home with Auntie Emm and Jonny on her knee and wrote to Dave.

'Let's get back to US I was just reading your letter again. Of course I remmber that rainey day, oh we did make love that night your defentley tastey. You can put some down sexy. Oh Dave I'm sorry if my letter upset you but *your all I can turn to*. Dave you said in your letter "I AM COMING BACK FOR YOU JOYSY" no matter what happens dont never let me down, *I love you Dave*. I hope and pray this parole comes out soon. No one will ever part us then will they. Dont worry about my birthday love your card from last year will go up on the shealf. Oh Dave hold on I go and get it. Do you no in aboat 10 years time were be down the country how many kids will be have remmber the night when we had a day dream in No 8 do you remmber? Who was going to make the bottle do you no what Im talking aboat we layed and pretended we had 6 was it? Come off it Joy. Oh no it wasent it was twins Oh Im getting carryed away now.

'Dave after the holiday I'm going to realy save for a car. Promise I must do some-thing to ockupine my mind.'

'Me roll-on's gone a dodgy colour – I put it in the Bendix.' Auntie Emm held up her corset. She wore a green quilted dressing gown, stained with egg down the front. She kept her stockings and roll-on under the settee cushion and took them out to put on before she went out.

And her rollers she kept in a biscuit tin under the sink. She hurried across the landing, feet turned out in a slightly bandy-legged walk, getting dressed. She takes out the pink plastic curlers and kicks off the mauve, velvet mules.

'I had it off with this Fred who keeps the fruit stall,

when you'd gone to bed last night. He's about seventy and when he went to give me a love bite, he lost his breath – he was heaving and puffing – it frit the life out of me.'

Joy got Jonny ready for bed. She took off his jumper and pressed it against her face and smelt the faintly milky smell, and felt with her cheek the part under the chin matted from his two-year-old dribble.

Outside the window, maroon trains push along the black grass embankment. The light grows dim, the smoke is white around the black engine and out of the funnel flies a red hot cloud.

The weeks go by; she holds the little boy in her arms and he leans against her humming a tune. Her heart ached and she didn't know why – she thought of Dave, and the long summer evenings together.

'He wants me to be like a nun but I'm not a nun – I don't feel like a nun,' she thought.

Gradually Joy got good at enjoying her men. She began to get really involved in sex – she could shut out who they were and what they looked like, and become a *femme fatále* for that night, geared up in her lacy underwear and false pony tail. She became a wild thing, lusty beneath the caress of Shelley.

He was a hairdresser – had three or four shops. I had it with him in his warehouse where he kept all his shampoo.

Five quid he gave me each time. I was on to a good thing there and he was only about sixty.

'Take your drawers off Joy there's a good girl.'

Proper lusty I was getting – it used to be love but it's all lust now – it's so terrific with different blokes. Sometimes you fancy it all soft and other times you want them to fuck the life out of you. Well you can't get that from the same bloke can you.

Beryl warned her: 'It's very dangerous this kinky scene, you get so caught up in it, so used to it you can't go back to being normal – doing it normally begins to mean nothing at all.'

But it was too late now.

'He said take yer drawers off – Heh that's probably where I caught me cold. Well I showed him me suspenders. We were standing in a hallway of an office block. Someone was coming and we ran down the basement stairs, the footsteps came on down and he pulled me into the Ladies, and inside one of the lavatories and locked the door – someone went in the other one then another girl comes and the two girls are having a conversation outside while me and him ... I had this crinoline lady's hairstyle. Oh I did look nice though I say it myself – I did look lovely ...

'I need different men to satisfy my different moods.'

*

And she thought of the young sailor, he was so thin and his knuckle bones stuck up like huge marbles in his hands, and the long stretched bones of his fingers.

There was one man she particularly liked. He was a gentleman, a professor of art or something like that, but he was young, in his thirties. Once when they were in a café together Joy had said of a picture on the wall – 'Oh isn't that a lovely picture. I don't understand art but I can feel it; and he said "You keep it like that it's better."' He hardly spoke himself, and she would chatter on and wonder why she reckoned him so much. Sometimes he said to her, 'You're a wonderful girl' and her heart would stand on end.

Once when they had crossed the road, a whirl of snow had risen up from the black gutter – he had the collar of his coat turned up around his neck and ears – a car skidded on the ice and he put both his arms round her. He never told her about his family. She asked him if he had children and he replied, 'Four', but he'd get her talking about hers, and bring her presents for Jonny. He never gave her money. He was a strange man – the most sensual she ever met, sensual and silent.

He would caress her for hours till her whole body had swooned away till her legs and thighs and spine had been washed away, till she no longer existed – he was the most complete and fantastic lover she ever had.

Then there was Petal again – with him it was quite different – unmixed with awe. Joy lay beside him on the candlewick bedspread, eating a soft buttered roll he'd saved specially for her from his round.

'I'm thinking of taking elocution lessons and becoming select.'

It was all right with Petal afterwards – he too was from Walham Green. But some of them they might have been from Mars for all the conversation she could have with them.

They told her they didn't have sex with their wives anymore – that their wives had let themselves go, got varicose veins and soft stomachs, or they were too wrapped up in their work. She just said, 'Oh, what a shame, love' and looked all sorry. Next minute she'd be touching them for money.

She was fascinated by the differences between her men, how one had small ears, almost like pearls, with drops of sweat gathering in the creases as she leant over him – and one enjoyed a certain caress and one enjoyed another, and she learnt them all. She learnt all the delicacies and different scents of her lovers. One smelt of sweet cigars, another of lilac deodorant, each mixed with their own sweat and skin. Like the Jewish boy – his broken nose and scarred face – 'I'm up at eight in the morning every day of my life – I only need four hours sleep. Business promotion that's what I'm in – start a business, get it going, then sell out and that way you build up capital.'

He put a pile of LP's on the radiogram – electric logs glowing in the fireplace, the expensive smell of aftershave lotion.

'I don't like being hard but you have to be in my business. I always regret it afterwards.'

Like fuck; thought Joy and touched him for a fiver.

He kissed me but it was horrible, his lips were too soft and I kept my eyes tight shut.

I've smoked weed and had Dave there with me – when really he's been away in prison. You have to keep your eyes closed, and he's there. You put on a record and you feel he's there, his arms round you – you really feel his arms, but then I open my eyes and see it's some dozy bloke with a hairdresser's shop in Peckham.

You've got to be careful sometimes, it's as if I'm hanging on all the time – just clinging on telling meself – life's all right – it's a great experience living – look at all the different people yer meeting – you really are living and then I think, Poor Cow, who are you taking on? Let's face it, it's just escaping from one misery to another. Who really enjoys life? Kids when you get down to it – kids are the only ones who really get a kick out of being alive – and then there was Mad Jack.

'I'm a real bachelor. I'm fifty-seven and I've never seen a woman in the nude – I guess they look like those statues in shop windows – that's what I think of when I give myself a thrill. If some woman would be kind enough to show me – she'd be doing me a great kindness.'

Joy sat in a low chair in the back room of his shop, with her skirt up above her knees one bare leg crossed over the other. He was a watchmaker from East Sheen.

'When it's dark I go out into the yard and rinse myself down in rainwater. I stand out there in the nude, or if it's very cold I keep me shoes on.'

He dropped a tiny spring on the floor by her feet and with his eye-glass clasped in his eye he got down on his hands and knees and searched, face close on the green and red lino.

A few days later, Auntie Emm told her, 'He called here for you and when I says you're out, "Out," he says, "in this weather – she'll catch her death without her drawers—"'

She and Jonny sat on the bed eating cornflakes. She leant against the wall and he sat cross-legged beside her, dipping his milky spoon in the bowl and splashing his bare legs. Then with his finger he'd rub the drop on his skin. When he'd had enough he began spitting small mouthfuls at his mother. She laughed when the spray hit her cheek so he got up on his knees and spat down her neck. 'Jonny,' she screeched, but he laughed louder, rolling back on the bed, his legs in the air. 'I spit Mama', he shouted. She put the bowls on the floor and buried her head in his stomach till he doubled up in an ecstasy of giggles, his eyes like huge chestnuts crumpled and creased into nothing, his wide mouth gasping for breath. 'Mama,' he said as he began to recover, 'do it again Mama! Again! Again!'

Even when she wasn't with him she could feel his weight in her arms and his mouth, after drinking, wet against her cheek – she thought of him as he raced in front of her down the road, feet splaying out like a runaway horse.

She wondered if it really made you any closer sleeping with someone – perhaps for a moment, when you cleave to their body but it doesn't last long. 'What's the use of worrying – I'm going to be an old woman before I'm a young one.'

Home with Auntie Emm she read out a knitting pattern. 'Neckband, I said six purl.'

She bent over to put more coal on the fire, her lovely round arse and narrow waist, and touching bare legs and thin feet in the bedroom slippers. Jonny lay on his stomach watching the terrapin in the glass jar, dipping in an occasional small finger.

'Help, where's me false hair – the dog ain't had it has he Auntie Emm? Oh.'

'There it is you silly cow.'

'Oh fuck me, hear me heart beating – I did get a fright.'

'Tell you what, Auntie Emm, Beryl knows this photographer what might give me a test to do modelling. What do yer think? I must have some sex-appeal somewhere but I wonder where?'

She wrote to Dave:

'... I think it because of you I so mental ill over what happens. I really am, its all coming out on me now. You see Dave Im so in love with you and having somebody like you, has made me notice all my mistakes. If I tryed explaining it to you it would take me all night. I love *You* so much in facket your killing me. I've never felt like this in my life, and thats why its affecting me all different ways, the doctor thinks it shock (Because Im a hypo) HA HA taking it all *in*. *I Love You Dave* and thats all that matters to me and you love me, were so mixed up its like a nightmare we keep pushing our way through every-day that passes I think to myself another day nearer to Dave it seems mad but everyday counts in facted every minute xxxx Oh I miss you very much darling, Oh I'm so frighten some think might happen to us. ('Joysy your tempting Providence Dont') Yes Dave I know but I'm so frighten. *I Love you Dave* and even if we cant have each other now were have each other in the END. I believe that and always will. I could never love anybody like I love You. And believe me being away from you is killing me our hole happiness gone down the drain for 12 years. Oh darling they killed something in us when they parted us.'

And underneath Dave wrote 'YOU POOR KID XXX.'

THE MODEL

'Saturday. You no when we go out and we met someone, nothing enters my head. I say good night and thats the finish. You can imagine what they think me and Beryl are ha ha. You no better than that. I fancey you to much time is nothing to us. *I love You Dave* ... if I had the chance I'll marry you right now. Yes right now, Dave.

'Well my love, I have something to tell you. ha ha. Me and Beryl have taken up Modeling ha ha Yes. Its alright nothing bad we get £2 an *hour* mind you only 1 hour a week so far, I'll send you some photos in my bikeny Sexy. Well what do you think———? new you wouldnt mind. So this week will be busy up the White Horse I'll be as thin as a rake I feel much better since I've worked up there. I can dress up makes me feel nice.

'I had my first test last Wednesday. Oh Dave you would never have thought it was me. By the way its for the

Revalie – Praded – Men Only, you never no you may open a paper and say that's that Joysy. I doesnt look like me I had a long pice of fals hair sexy, not bad at all, bottom of my bekiny black top. Black neglegee with Green nylon Night-dress – Oh its all mad realy. Top hat was the funniest he said I could have some of the photoes so shall I send them to You. Yes Joysy of course still musent let it go to my head A. Mind you the lights are so briliont.

'I bought a new dress (on Book) its nice moden (Brown and White) Dave if my divorse come through I'll marry you straite away I promise you that.

'Well love what do you think of your "Joysy" as a modle?'

Beryl and Joy trooped along the road, it was raining. The smell of fish drifted out of a café onto the wet street. It was to be Joy's first nude night.

'I'm nervous Beryl, I can feel meself sweating – I'm sure I stink.'

'It's all right, as soon as he finishes taking the photo he drapes you over with a cloth – he's a headmaster to some boys' school – he's not a dirty old man.

'You're like me I suffered terribly with my nerves years ago and I had absolutely no confidence. If I walked up the steps on to the top of a bus I thought the person behind me was criticising my arse. My friend advised me to become a figure model – she said once you've taken your clothes off the first time you'll find it much easier the second.

'The first time I done it I saw this advert, in a newsagent's in Piccadilly. I was only seventeen at the time and earning three pound a week as a shop assistant. I phoned the man up – he told me he'd meet me in this café and I'd know him because he'd be wearing a mac with a flower in the buttonhole. Well when he saw me he said he'd like to give me the job and he'd pay me a pound an hour. He took me off to the Regent Palace Hotel and we sat in the lounge all prim and had a cup of tea. We went up in the lift after and I felt ever so embarrassed thinking everyone was looking at me. We goes into this big posh bedroom and he says to me take all your clothes off except your suspender belt and stockings, he liked the active type of poses. Well I met him every week. Of course he tried once or twice to touch me but he was a mild little man and I brushed him away like you would a fly. I took it very seriously, I mean I was earning a pound an hour, I'd never heard of earning money like that at seventeen. I was a bit slow too or I probably could have got a lot more out of him.'

The summer evening melts into dusk down the North End Road, and the voices of children float up to the open window. Inside the room is brilliantly lit with floods and spots and boomlights and Courtenay-Major II Power-Pack 1250 joules.

'Here, let's toss up who's going to be the first one.'

'You go first. Last time I wore a sari and held a camel whip. One bloke, I think he was pissed or had DT's, he was shaking so much.'

'The models that we've secured tonight without regard to expense are Joy and Beryl – they'll pose this way and that and how's your father. Any advice for beginners will be gladly given.'

Joy appears, with a couple of whistles, in transparent black with a cigarette burn in the front.

'So I want piles and piles of bright ideas from you lads tonight.'

Out comes a measuring stick. Joy holds one end against her sweet flesh. Tripods growing like a forest. Clicking and, 'your turn next'. Joy loops her fox fur under her glowing bum. Then she whisks it over her shoulder and under one breast. She's really getting into the swing and feeling – this is what I was born for – this is my vocation.

'Give me a nasty dirty look as though I'm the lowest form of life.' He lies full length below her, in his braces as if on the beach at Blackpool.

'Oh my gawd,' thinks Joy, 'whatever next.' He is fat and short, she is long-limbed and skinny. There is talcum powder in her navel. She licks her finger and rubs at a pink spill on the black nylon.

'Drop your straps sweetie. That's it, bless you, and again looking down your nose this time.'

'Now can you repeat the line of your thigh with the line of your arms – that's it thank you my sweet.'

Now Beryl comes in nude. 'Have you a hat with you, dear?'

'Pretend there's loads of sun and you're soaking it up.'

'If any of the gentlemen want any fishing nets or baskets sing out.'

'Just a nasty face over your shoulder.'

In the hurry two men collide. Now they put Joy in the most excruciating position.

'Look natural dear.' 'Don't make her sit on the wicker it'll mark her.' 'Wait a moment I'll get the leopard skin.' A bit of nylon leopard is produced from the back. 'But the stool flattens her sit-upon.'

'Now hold your shoes dear and yawn just as if you was all ready for bed.' He cocks his Brownie on one side and snaps it. 'God bless you.'

A tray of coffee and biscuits is brought in and Joy and Beryl go behind a curtain. Above is a notice, PHOTOGRAPHERS PLEASE KEEP AWAY WHILE MODEL IS CHANGING.

Joy walked home along the tow path and watched the wild swans flying in formation over the iron bridge. A bird sat in a dripping, shivering silver birch.

'You don't want to stay there mate you'll catch pneumonia,' said Joy. She wondered if she'd go to heaven. 'I believe in God. I think he's very big like in the Bible and he's got a long beard. I hope I go to heaven.'

JOY TAKES THE TEST

Her body developed into a highly sensitive machine; she noticed the colour of leaves and felt her bare thighs touching where she wore no stockings. She noticed the faint dust on men's bare backs on building sites. When stripped before the cameras she was a queen.

Well, I love flaunting in the nude put it that way. Tom used to say no one would have me, you know, 'I don't know what's lovely about you', but now I know there is something about me. Because the bloke wouldn't phone me up otherwise. There's nothing crooked in it. It's not nothing perverted. Not pornographic pictures, nothing like that.

She had a call-box put in in the passage at Auntie Emm's – men phoned her up and Auntie Emm put on her toff voice and took messages. One day she caught Bet, the nutcase in the room above, leaning over the banisters listening.

'Here you, this is a private conversation, what d'you think you're doing?'

She came down the stairs with a broom, her red hair falling round her face in sausage curls, one hand on her hip she faced Auntie Emm.

'I'm phoning the landlord, tell him you used my floor-cloth to wipe the passage with.'

Emm held the phone in one hand threateningly.

'You do that and I'll knock you over the head with this instrument – why didn't they keep you locked up you barmy old cow.'

Bet ran at her, using the broomstick as a harpoon and shrieking like a warrior. Aunt Emm dodged and the broom hit the door of the bathroom with a shattering of glass. Joy came running up the stairs.

'What on earth's going on? This is like a mad house, this is.' Jonny stood in the doorway and Joy caught him up in her arms. 'Come in Aunt Emm, I'm closing the door. Get upstairs Bet, this is our landing.'

'I'm phoning the landlord.'

'Get upstairs or I'll be phoning the asylum and have you put away. You're not just cranky, yer fucking mad.'

Bet scuttled up the stairs and Emm went in muttering to herself, 'Why do I always end up in a place packed with nutcases – there's a man on the top floor – all he does is type all day, tip-tap, tip-tap, enough to drive anyone round the bend.'

'If they're not there already,' said Joy as she took the little boy on her knee.

'Shall we go to the swings Jonny?'

And he ran across the floor and got his boots from the corner. 'Boots! Boots!' he chanted.

As she pushed his small body in the swing till he flew up towards the trees – higher and higher, safe in the little wooden chair up, up, his head dizzy with the height, his hair blowing first forward and then back as he swung to and fro – she thought of Petal.

Petal was all right. Petal was definitely lusty. He took me to this hotel, opposite Brixton Prison – Transport House it was called. 'We'll just skate in here,' he'd say, 'and have a bit of a lie down.' I remember the wallpaper it was bright yellow with these little Chinese pagodas and weeping willows stuck all over it. He strokes the inside of my legs till I'm all lit up – he has these fingers like magic they was. Men are terrific – it's not only for sex. You can talk to them. If you talk to women they don't never really understand you. If you talk to women all you listen to is what they done yesterday and what they're going to do tomorrow.

But sometimes if I hadn't had it for two or three weeks I can be really frightened to get undressed, that's why I like to have it often. It's very embarrassing. I don't care if I've got fancy clothes on and they look at me lusty, then I don't mind but if you wear ordinary things like white pants and white brassieres they think 'Oh, whoever does she think she is?' Really they do. In sex, when you have it with somebody, you think they're not looking, you think Oh God, they're only waiting for me to get in bed and have it, instead of that they're comparing you, comparing you with someone else. They want to have sex because they know it's wrong, they're stealing someone else's food. Take one fellow. I got into bed with him and I don't get nothing out of it. I can't come at all. It puts me off. I think, Well, he only wants me for my body, he don't want me for meself. So I get remorse. I get terrible now. I think, Oh fuck him, I don't want to have it with him, and we're halfway there. And he says 'Are you coming, are you coming? And I go all bent on it. And I say, 'No, I can't come.' Honest to God I do really. I go quite dead on him and I'm thinking all the time about how I'd like to be married.

Long white dress, long blonde hair and loads of flowers. And I'd like him to say, 'Well this is my wife.' And I'd like a good drink and go on a long honeymoon. I still dream a bit, I am a dreamer. Trouble is I open my fucking eyes and I'm in a warehouse in Cable Street, lying on a pile of fucking packing – you know that wood shaving stuff they use to pack bottles in. I'm lying on a ton of that surrounded by bottles of shampoo and pink plastic rollers and a load of hairpins – and I think, Come to Joy, whatever are you doing here? Anyway after we'd had it he gave me two nylon overalls, navy blue – ever so nice like they wear in the hairdressers' shops, so he wasn't too bad really.

She wrote to Dave:

'I'm taking your advice working hard to try to forget it helps a little bit. But in my heart I dont want to forget because its to easy that way. If youve got to suffer I want to. I *have got* to feel like you do. Got 3 new Jumper 1 black pair of tites Oh they look good you never guess how much £13 10. 0 on the book still must have some things on my holidays brought Jonny his first bike, he rides it round the room bumping into Auntie Emm. Oh Dave I'm mad. I'm rushing with this letter I've got my driving lesson in a minute. Next week I go for my test. I am nerves, I'll get a book from the library on the car then when I've saved up to buy it I be able to come every month without fail – really am going to do it – its for you in one way so your have a visit as much as I can. I show you Dave – I can do it for us. So darling you'll have to help me – have faith in me.'

It was a rotten wet morning the day I went for me test. I sat in the little waiting room sick with nerves – supposing the arrangement had gone wrong and they'd given me the wrong bloke. I've given meself a spring clean – all clean, bra, drawers, the lot so if he does want to take me home ...

It was an enormous bloke with a bushy red moustache what called my name.

'Mrs Steadman.' I jumped up a mile as if a bee had stung me – then up I get bold as brass.

We's walking along the road to the car and I'm chatting him up like a mad thing not even certain if he's the right one.

'Now before you get in I've got to warn you I haven't had much practice.' He doesn't even laugh – his eyes go steely behind his glasses – fuck me this can't be him I'm thinking. So in he gets. The window's jammed open his side, so I've brought this rug. I got it off the back seat and tucked it over his knees – 'here get this round you in case you catch a chill.'

'No thank you, Mrs Steadman,' he says.

'You're not going to get up to no tricks while we're going along are you – I don't want to crash me mate's car.'

'I'll give you plenty of warning, you've only to follow my instructions,' he says.

'Oh, I'll do that all right – I'm ever so good at following instructions.'

I swing round the corner and only miss a bleedin' parked car, while Bushy Moustache mops his brow.

'Now will you pull up at the end of this road, and proceed to do a three-point turn.'

'A three-point what?' I says.

'A three-point turn, if you please, Mrs Steadman,' he says.

'Like my jumper? I bought it at a jumble sale in Putney, a shilling, it's ever so select in Putney.'

Then I only stalled in the middle of my three-point turn. 'Here,' I says, 'get it in reverse for me.'

I'm stuck there in the middle of the road. The rain's pissing down blowing in through the winder misting up his glasses.

'Oh this bleeding rotten poxy car – me mate warned me the gear was stiff but I never knew the poxy thing was as bad as this.'

I felt a bit sorry for him really. There's me with me skirt hitched up and him trying to get the gear in – and not knowing if he wants a little bit or not. I felt like saying, 'What about stopping for a nice cup of tea?' Perhaps somewhere along the line someone bungled it – or perhaps he didn't fancy me, anyway he says at the end: 'I'm sorry Mrs Steadman but I can't pass you, next time you take yer test take it in a car you understand.'

'I'm sorry too love,' I said. In fact I'm really choked. And I was, I could feel the tears come into my eyes. What a balls up!

Once a week Beryl and Joy went modelling – they hurried along the street together as the sun set over the Power

Station and girls emptied out of the factories smelling of sweat. They go home stinking of sweat and scrub and change their drawers and leave smelling of hairspray and Coty perfume.

Joy with her bleached blonde ponytail dangling over her shoulder, her skinny legs in the high heeled elasticated, suede boots, her small mouth and boot-button eyes with the thick, clustering 'real-hair' eyelashes and Cleopatra curls over her ears, her skinny body and her large breasts.

She sees a rack of bargain shoes across the high street. 'Look Beryl,' she shrieks dragging her in and out of cars. The cheap, crappy shoes, like stars, beckoning from the other side of the road, she rushes along the rack trying them all on her skinny foot tossing off her black suede boot for Beryl to hold. She picks them off the rack. 'A pound, they're only a pound,' and hops about on one leg as she tries them on on the pavement hopping about and trying first the pale-blue suede with the bow, the satin bow slightly dusty from the high street. 'I'll soon rub 'em up.' 'Do you think they look sexy? I'll get a black dress tighter than tight to wear with them, low cut black dress and what coat – oh I haven't got a coat. Sure these are the best?' She picks out some red ones, with plastic ankle straps, thin red cords round her bony ankles making her look like an abandoned waif on a station platform. And Beryl, the big sort, would march beside her, dainty in spite of all her flesh.

'When my mum was carrying me she went with a German bloke and that's why I go a bit mad now and again, I've got a wicked temper – that's true I was a mixed baby. Do you know you can fall with a white man and have it with a coloured bloke when you're carrying and it'll turn out a half-caste?'

They pass a huge neon sign of some red gums with white teeth, and underneath, REPAIRS.

'Dirty Bertie, he had this white Jaguar – he gave me a quid here and there. Other blokes – I get them out of their misery, play games with them for nothing. I wear me black jumper with the holes in it and pull me brassieres up round me neck. You know Big Harry what comes in the pub – he's nineteen stone, he's got a caravan and an Alsatian dog. He divorced his first wife and he lost his second wife and now he wants to settle down, but he's as scruffy as hell. Have a little bit with him and that'd be my lot with nineteen stone on top of me – oh no he's too big.

'I'm getting engaged to the other one – he's buying me an engagement ring and he's going to marry me three months after his wife dies – she's got a weak heart. I could do with his savings – I had a row with him the other night. Called me all the bastards. "Get up there you whore," he says. Life's one big gamble. You've got to take what you can out of it – it won't come to you – trouble is I haven't found anyone worth taking yet.

'It's no use gettin married – all you do is go home and

listen to the old man – "Oh I have worked hard today Beryl" and I say "Here's yer dinner love" – once they're married all they want to do is sit in front of the telly and eat cheese rolls.'

That evening there was quite a crowd of amateur photographers armed with Brownies to greet Beryl and Joy – they were getting well known as 'the double event', they'd even had a mention in *Nude Photography for the Common Man*.

There was this long pole and you had to stand with your back leaning against it this side and Beryl the other side. Well, Beryl goes and puts her whole weight against it and the pole falls over bang smash! And we both go down wallop. It frightened the guts out of me, I thought, Oh my God have they seen more than they should? You can get done for that – showing yerself in public – yeah it's all very strict, there's a white line between the photographer and the model and if one of them steps over that line they can get done for it.

But it's a marvellous feeling to see them all out there clicking away. I'd like to get my photo in the *Parade*, it would be the best thing that had ever happened to me.

Sometimes me and Beryl would get blocked round her place. Once we thought we was two Arab girls and we done this wonderful dance in the nude. And sometimes I lie back when I've had a smoke and I can feel Dave there with me – really felt him touching me, holding me in his arms. I put on our record, 'Stand By Me' and he's there, all around me and it's the chandelier night, it was all like sparklers, like crystals falling on yer – it was so pretty – I'll never forget that night as long as I live.

Coming home late one evening, the shops closed, their affluent goods lit up and the rain running down the thick glass, she came to Fulham Broadway. In a telephone kiosk, at one o'clock in the morning, lay a woman.

'Are you all right?' says Joy opening the door. 'Yes, I sleep here every night.' She was crumpled under the telephone, eyes wide open, dirty tweed coat, bare legs and white sandals.

'What'll she do when the winter comes?' thought Joy and wondered desperately how she could find a genuine man of position. But when she was with a man – even a man with certain prospects, she thought:

'I try to forget there's anything to me – I listen to his problems, his moans and groans then he gets undressed and I look at his body and smell the smell of his skin and I think suddenly what am I doing here with this horrible old bastard – why aren't I at home with my little Jonny and his lovely limbs and hair and feet and sweet smell? Here I am touching up this dirty old man for a couple of quid when my Jonny's at home with his cod-liver oil breath.'

MEMORIES

She wrote to Dave:
    'Dave do you remmber the Punch and Judy Show at Blackpool? and you put 2/6 instead of 2d. Ha ha. Oh darling I must clos now as I'm going to curl my hair up love you darling Dave my colds worse "RED NOSE" HA HA. keep sniffing. My eyes are running (Oh I should be in bed), and I havent been sitting in drafs. I do feel a bit ruff still I muson conmplain. Im going to miss you more … Tom comes out in 3 months but I shan't go back to him – I'll keep on with the divorse. Dont worrie our time will come one day have pations. Remmber you making that fort for Jonny and *Making* me go and pick branches Oh Dave your a rotter ha ha and brushing my nose (hold your head down) still I loved it, we did have some lovely times. Dave just thought of this remmber that Posh Restrant? I think it was in Wales? do you remember it and it was a bit to posh for us and I said our moneys as good as theres ha

ha. I had that big green cardgian on I think Ha. Remmber that midnight walk you took me for and we see the star move, I forgot to tell you that. I remember us trying to have it in the car do you remember? I only like it in confort and staying at the Hotel, and me worrie about the sheets and you taking the nail brush. I was thinking of been a *nurse*, would I make a good one, as your always saying I'm so Wimsercal. xxxx

'Dave I fill terrible tiered, if you were sitting beside me I could put my head on your shoulder and go fast asleep. Oh Wake up Joy come back to life still its nice to imagine it. Dave do you remmber the Biddies you used to talk about well they made me a bit Jeolose at times. By the way Eve may have been formey, but she had bad teeth.'

Out of the window a black and white cat walked up a plank of wood and sat on a gravestone looking about him – there was a tree in the next garden, a big tree with spreading branches. They were going to cut it down, Auntie Emm said, because it had too many leaves.

She thought of her last night's modelling – black top hat, a cane and a scarf, very sexy, she'd thought at the time, but the thought of it now depressed her, as did Petal.

All the things I loved him for now get on my nerves. When he used to smile – I used to think his crooked teeth were marvellous – now I think how ugly and crooked they are. And his clothes – I used to think his clothes were great, now I think they're flash and ugly and he was wearing this ridiculous pair of shoes, I was embarrassed to walk down the road with him.

He phoned me up – I knew what he wanted. 'No' I said, 'I've got a terrible cold.' 'I'll buy you a box of pills,' he said. 'Fucking cheek,' I said. 'Is that all you're going to give me?'

I don't know what's the matter with these blokes, they don't realise what they've got now. If they've got a good wife they don't want it. They should have women that are right no-good and they would think a bit more of their wives.

And she went up the solicitor's again, trooped up the gloomy, narrow staircase, with the glass door at the top. The girl receptionist in her tight jumper went on talking to the typist and sipping her tea. Joy stood there furious.

'Yes please,' she said, taking a final gulp and crashing down her cup in the chipped saucer.

Joy sat in the chair and looked at the solicitor. He had a smooth face and a grey suit. 'How can I ever get through to him,' she wondered.

'No he didn't have a job – he gave me what he earned.'
'You mean illicitly.'
'What does that mean?'

The man shifted in his chair and wrote on a large sheet of paper, with 'Steadman' on the top right hand corner.

'I'm working at this pub but I can't go every day because of my little boy. I have a fiver a week, and I make it do, I mean one club one week and when I've paid that up it's my turn and then it's Jonny's turn and then it's my turn.'

'So really you exist, you live on five pounds a week?' the solicitor looked at her amazed.

'Mm. People never believe it. I mean the little luxuries I have is if I meet a bloke and he gives me a couple of quid.'

'He gives you a couple of quid. I see Mrs Steadman.'

'That's it yes. So that to me is marvellous, you know what I mean. Like when I went out and he gave me a fiver. And I come home and what did I buy? I bought a couple of little bits and pieces, bought Jonny a pair of shoes. Jonny never goes without anything, I had a beautiful Persian lamb once what Tom brought me and my little John wanted this bike. Tom was away at the time and I never had a penny. I didn't honestly. I sold my Persian lamb for fifty bob so he could have this bike. That's the truth, well fifty-nine bob it was. Mind you it broke my heart – and every time I see this girl in my coat I could fuckin' kill her. I could really. Loads of things I sold yet. So that my little Jonny could have it. I mean if he come in and the kids go up the fair it may be my last six bob I'll give 'im four of that. I do. I regret it. I don't want to but I give it to him because the other kids got it. You know, the other kids have got money and he hasn't got it. He never wanted for a thing, all the time his father's been away, I can swear to it.'

'Do you like dressing up and looking smart Mrs Steadman?'

'Oh yes, call me Joy, it makes me nervous being called Mrs Steadman. Mm. Always have done. I must never change because that's my one pride I've got. If I haven't got nothing else I like to dress up, or touch my roots up in my hair. And I really like to look nice.'

'I see,' and he wrote on his paper.

'My mother-in-law's a big woman – I was frightened of her – she hit me once. Well what I say is if you can't beat 'em, join 'em. Yes, I haven't got no peace of mind. I'm here today and gone tomorrow. Oh it's fucking potty. And love is really the most important thing, don't you think Mr Pinker? Love. Happiness is the most important thing. Love and happiness. Money isn't. In my life now I only want money. 'Cos I've got nothing else. I mean I can't have Dave. Though work has never worried me, no I don't mind working. I like helping people. Even Dave used to tell me, you know he'd have his little game with me in that way. If someone said "Oh I'll have that Joy," I'd give it to them, never think if I wanted it. I'm potty. I'll never change. I bought a dress off this woman, it was a beautiful dress and my cousin liked it and she never had much. I said, "You can have it." But I didn't tell Dave and I put it in a carrier bag and I pretended I never knew about it. And he found out about it. Does your wife like to dress up, Mr Pinker?'

Mr Pinker allowed an icy smile to flicker across his lips, but he vouchsafed no answer.

Later, in the pub it was hot. Joy sprayed body mist under her arms every hour – she knew the sort of barmaid in the black frock that stank as she pulled the beer.

'Do you think them sort of people ever really know trouble?' she asked Beryl.

'In the upper classes you can get around, that's the best thing about the upper classes. But there are a lot of people that have got plenty of money and would like to be like us – go out, have a good time, but they can't – they have to be careful over the people they mix with.

'I've heard it said there's as many abortions among that sort of person as there is among us – though they don't use the same methods.'

Joy rubbed the glasses.

'I thought of putting an advert in the paper. "Model 22 with 2 year old son wants a week's holiday, go anywhere, do anything. Age not objected to".'

'Me friend, Gabby, you know the one, she's bin in here. Well, she got caught last month. She done it herself. She used potash. You put it on a tampax and put it up inside you and it burns it out of you – this little baby come out with its arms and legs all burnt up one side. When you stop to think, how lucky you are!'

'Oh Beryl yer making my guts turn over – I helped someone once, I'll never forget it as long as I live.

'She'd just had one baby – and they only had a single room, he was about a year, I think, and she phoned me up and she said, "Joy, I've had it done, will you come over." 'Course me, silly cow, went over didn't I, and she only lived in one room then. Then I went with her and we had mincemeat this day, I cooked the dinner, 'cos she said, "I'm having terrible pain", and I thought well I can't leave her, although not realising what sort of trouble I could have got into. So I thought well I'll stay here. And then oh, little Jonny had gone to sleep on the studio couch and her husband was laying down with my little Jonny and the baby was asleep, it was one o'clock in the night, well one o'clock in the morning, you know, and suddenly she said, "I've got backache Joy", and fucking-well grabbed hold of me, frit the guts out of me. I'm saying, "What's the matter, what's the matter?" I didn't know what was what. And I've never seen one and she says have a look, and you know how you have a look, so I looked to see if she was all right and all of a sudden there was – you know she was sitting on the bucket like that and all of a sudden there was blood coming and I looked inside to see if she was all right and it was like the baby's head. It was horrible, yes, it was about that big, I'm not telling no lies it really was. And the head come and the legs, I don't know if it was the legs first. Anyway it was hanging from her, I'll never forget it as long as I live, to me it seemed like ten years, she was holding on to me and she was sitting on this tin bucket, and she was sitting there and you could tell she was in pain – she was grabbing hold of me and moaning the most terrible moan like an animal.'

'What was her husband doing?'

'He was saying, "Are you all right?" Then all of a sudden plop, it fell in, it was in the bucket then.'

'Christ, it must have turned your guts up.'

'It did, it did, so I mean really I should be turned off of blokes by now. It was a little boy, it had a little Willie, it did honest, it had little eyes. Anyway her husband went out so I said, "What you going to do with it?" 'Cos I couldn't touch it, I couldn't touch nothing like that. I don't believe in nothing like that. Anyway he put it down the toilet and she was sick, oh she was bad, anyway I washed her, and she started shivering then so we put her in bed and made a cup of tea for her, and then he done that with the baby and that was it. I went out the next day and got a bottle of peppermint cordial so I give her a little drop and put some boiling water in it, that'd clean her. It is good, it don't matter where you are, if you got a cold or anything and I give her a wash, see that the baby was washed and dressed and got the dinner ready for her and she laid in bed and I went home.'

And to Dave she wrote:

'Do you remember Norfolk, all our memories started

there and you liked it so much and you was happy, I can imagin you and me sitting on the wall near where you stayed last year we cuddled. Oh it was so nice, Jonny picked me some Daisys, but we never took no photos. Still not to worrie we could lose our photos but not our memories we've got them for *ever* and *ever*.

'Oh my love please dont worrie, I thought of you so much today it realy hurt me to know way down deep inside of you you have really given up but Rember Dave. I Love You. Oh Dave so much in facked the love for you is killing me every day I fill a big lump in my froat leaving you behind. Oh darling what can we do. Stick-to-gether through thick and thin. Thats your Joy, and she will but I need you and all your love. Its going to be so hard so very hard but your the only one who I realy want to MARRY TO LOVE. Things will change as years go by but I'll never marry any one else, I MEAN THAT (even if they did have plenty Money House Car) they could never have what you have.'

STILL DREAMING

Joy had blossomed and bloomed since she began her modelling. She walked along with her head up and her white skin freckled from the sun, over her shoulder hung her pony-tail newly washed and shiny. She'd plaited it up and tied the end with a blue ribbon. She wore a dolly dress she'd got off her tally man the day before – it was short and green, and cotton.

'I want to be liquid, mobile, like that fairy in the panto,' she thought. 'Tinker Bell wasn't she called? All lovely and moving about how she fancied, and yet can I do it?'

She was taking her urine up to the hospital to be tested. She'd had strange pains in her stomach lately and wondered if she had an ulcer. Beryl was with her, dressed in black though the sun shone, with a diamond clasp on her left breast. She took small steps and the little gold chain round her ankle bounced up and down.

'Of course that's it, being respectable makes it all much

simpler. You can lie in bed and eat chocolates all day once you've got a bloke bringing you home twenty quid a week.'

'That's it,' said Joy. As they walked through the back streets paper blew about on the broken pavement. Someone was having a bonfire in their front garden, it was blazing red and yellow and a woman with an Indian-brown face threw on worm-eaten table legs.

'When I was on holiday in Folkestone we met two fellers. They were quiet fellers but really respectable – my mum was with me and I wondered if this was me chance to play it innocent and get meself a husband.'

Big Beryl adjusted her bra. 'Me tits haven't half come up lovely and firm since I went on the pill, Joy, me arse has got bigger too, I can't pull my breasts up, that's my only downfall, if I pull them up they strangle me but I like to know I've got them.

'My sister's getting married. We haven't seen him yet, but she says he's fifteen stone and pock-marked. I was with me brother the other night, his girl friend catches him looking at Joany's legs, so she goes mad, bang goes the table up in the air. She gets hold of him. He goes to hit her, my gawd, crash go all the cups and saucers. But she was quite right, he was lookin' at Joany's legs ... but there again sometimes you wonder if that's being respectable, not looking at other people's legs, well bollocks to respectability.

'And you sit there and listen to them and my sister-in-law says, "I gave him chocolate pudding for afters on

Saturday, a change is as good as a rest any day of the year," and I think to meself what do you know about change.'

A street is being demolished and tattered human debris lies in the once tended front gardens – mouldering mattresses, battered chairs and rusting saucepans, put by for the totters who never came.

'I definitely don't want to stay in my own class, I want to go up in the world – I want a position – I'm going to classes on how to speak properly and how to approach people – that's very important you know Joy – the right approach.'

'Yeah I dare say, she's always drumming it into me that I'll end as nothing, my Auntie – "Ye'll end up like me Joysy, one foot in the grave and the other in the gutter." I wish I could find a well-off bloke – you can always tell if they've got money, even without their clothes on. One day I'm going to have a wine-coloured car.'

They go into a chemist and see a tray marked PERFUME SALE. Little bottles of green and yellow scent.

'Here Beryl, only ninepence. I'm having three bottles – "Sweet Love", oh yeah that's me – "Harvest Sensation", that's you and "Magic Moment" that's for both of us when we're blocked.' They go out into the road laughing, Beryl, one big arm round Joy's small neck to support her in her giggles. 'Oh dear, smells like lemonade powder.'

'I used to have a mate called Ivy. We dyed our hair pink, there was a record out "My little runaway". I had me eyebrows shaved off – that was the fashion those days and

I had these eyebrows pencilled on right up me forehead – I was a common cow. She was dark, I was fair – the blokes used to call us the Dolly Sisters.

'It was that hot summer, I was a waitress at a holiday camp. It was like a brothel.'

'That's it, I went on this outing. There were thirty of us – all blondes. I've got the photo indoors. We went on the Mickey Mouse at Southend, and he started screaming. I thought "I'm with a dopey bloke here." On the way home one of the girls hangs her drawers in the back window, common cow she was, and I stuck a sticker next to them WE'RE ON OUR WAY TO BILLY GRAHAM. We swopped half our coach with a men's outing from Hackney and we was snogging all the way back from Southend. I bought a pair of green sling backs. Oh they were beautiful, oh they did look lovely.'

'But deep down I'll tell you something. I'm very unhappy. He only wanted me, and no-one else. They gave him twelve years. Dave, I truly love him. He'd give you the world with one hand and take it back with the other. Once when I'd had a ruck with him, he got hold of this three quid and lit it with a match and on my life he burnt it – I never knew he thought that much of me. I love being possessed. That's what I liked about Dave – and you could have it when you wanted – oh, if only he hadn't got nicked. When I went to see him last month he puts his leg against you and you can feel the heat, then you drop something on the floor and I bent down and pushed my hand against him and I can feel myself throbbing. But he's losing his hair, Beryl, and his eyes have gone all sad on him.

'I wish I could sort it all out. Will it ever get sorted out? Tom wants me to go back with him – but I'm sick to death of tea leaves – do you think I should go back to him, Beryl? He comes home next week. He's wrote to me, says he's changed, he says we'll move right away down to the country. He knows someone in Rochester who's offered him a job down there, he expects me to live in a furnished room. "O", I wrote back, "I can't go down there in this weather, I'd freeze". I'm fed up with living in buggy places, I want a house, a nice house – I've got nothing – fuck all. When I was living in Fulham with Tom before the baby was born, I got the scabies through the bugs and had to go and be fumigated – they put you in a warm bath and then they paint you with white stuff. It burns and it smells terrible. No-one can take me dreams away from me – if I really push myself. If I really try I will get somewhere won't I?'

'Here Joy, look at that gorgeous bloke.' He sat in a car at the lights, jaunty pork-pie on his head and a little bristling moustache, he leant his elbow out the car window and smiled at the two girls.

'Give us a lift,' said Joy.

'Sorry love, I'm in a hurry.'

'Then lend us ten quid for an abortion,' shouts Beryl as he draws away.

'Funny how you get to know the way blokes like it. See him' – a man in braces and a jacket over his arm walked towards them – 'he's a proper Dad – not interested. Now him, he'd love it but he'd be scared stiff.' A small man darted out of a shop and passed the girls. 'You'd love it, wouldn't you Blossom?' Beryl calls after him and he scuttles away. A song came out of an open window.

Stay stay stay with me
Baby baby baby baby.

Joy walked jauntily. 'Sometimes, music, I'm with it – it's all around me.'

'You see, now I can walk down the street and look at the men, and I know they'd hold very few surprises,' says Beryl. 'Look at him. He's the kind that murder you first then hang you upside down in the wardrobe before he had anything to do with you. As for him you'd have to give him a good scrub before you touched him.'

'All the girls I see – they look so soft compared to me ... Why do I look hard, I didn't used ter.'

'I never give that nightdress to Barbara – well I was lying in bed and I'd got a friend coming to see me, so I couldn't lie there in the nude could I?'

'You know my Jonny – he was an act of God baby. Act

of God baby they call it, he was born in four minutes – without a warning.'

'Here Joy, belt up and take a look over there – Cor!' Two men in their forties sat in an open sports car – flash tweed suits, faces of measured corpulence. 'Wow, I bet they're worth a bit! That one at the wheel, that's the sort I could really tease – sometimes if they want the other, you know, I like to get them at it and when I get them at it I don't give it to 'em. I get a good result on it, you know. Especially when I kiss them goodnight and they think, Oh I could give 'er one. And I think, Oh, fuck 'em. That's what I think afterwards, fuck them, that's all they wanted out of me.'

'That was Shelley the hairdresser, he'd make me get undressed then he'd tap me bum and I'd jump up in the air and say, oooh. Then he'd say, "You have a little comey!" It makes you feel sick but as I said the money comes in handy.

'They ought to call me Lust-pot, yeh, that would be a good name for me. Lustpot Lynne from the Elephant and Castle. Once I went in a train to the country and I saw an engine standing in a siding beside a flooded meadow – everywhere is water. It was lovely Beryl.'

'You're too soft Joy, that's the trouble with you – what with your Jonny and yer cottage in the country you'll never make it – you give it away as often as not – admit it – you give it away don't you?'

'Don't you ever, Beryl?'

'Well last night I took this bloke home from the pub

and gave him a wank. Should be one guinea but I only charged him a pound – Yeah it's usually a pound for her and a shilling for the maid – even if you haven't got one. They're not to know are they?

'So I let him have it cheap really – but I couldn't let 'em have it fer nothing – I'd feel degraded – I'd feel they were taking me on.'

They walked through the main gate of the enormous hospital; neat hollyhocks grew in circles and a notice said PLEASE DO NOT PICK THE FLOWERS.

'I wonder where we should go. Shall we try Casualty?'

'Yes,' says the porter.

'Oh good afternoon,' says Joy – 'I've brought me water – the doctor told me.' The porter looked puzzled and she opens her bag and holds up the little bottle.

'Oh it's not Casualty you want, it's the Path. lab. over there.'

'So sorry,' she said.

'You cow,' said Beryl. 'Of course they wouldn't want yer water in Casualty – that's for road accidents.'

It was sunny and a lot of the patients were out of doors in wheelchairs.

'Some of the things you see you wonder how they can bear to live.'

An old woman all skin and bone with a huge protruding belly sat under a tree.

'She's got fluid on the stomach by the looks of her –

she's so ill she just doesn't care – she don't care about nothing – think of ending up like that.'

'I once went for a nursing job. The matron says to me, "You must be strict, don't make a fuss of them". "Well maybe they want a little fuss – they probably haven't got no home life", I says. One old man of ninety taps me on the arse with his stick. "Hello nurse" – he was having a false lip and a moustache put on ... but I only stuck it for a week.'

Joy gave up her bottle through a small hatch and on the way out they peeped through an open door – there were shelves of big glass jars, identical to the jars full of Jelly Babies and Dolly Mixtures in the corner shop, but inside them floated grey abominations. On the labels she read 'KEEP' in big letters, and underneath, in Biro, 'Heart G Paterson 12/8/64 – and 'Kidneys C Bailey 10/2/63'. 'Poor geezers, how are they going on with bits missing – I suppose they've made them out of plastic or rubber. They can't be dead or they would of had to bury them.'

'Oh you never know these days. There was this young girl we all knew very well and she was killed in a car accident and we went to her funeral – we were all standing there and round the corner comes the parson carrying a little brass urn, just a little urn and a few days ago she was a fourteen-year-old tomboy running and jumping about.'

'Oh Beryl, I'm frightened to die, definitely frightened. I'd hate to die young. If I had an illness – if I died, you realise I've got nothing, I'm leaving all what I've got behind. Jonny,

Dave, even Tom. I want to go to heaven. Well, I don't really, but when I come to think of it I'd hate to go to hell. That's where I'll end up – that's where they'll send me, down there.'

'What do you imagine it's like in heaven, Joy?'

'In heaven? I think it's all white. Everything's white there. You're purer then. You start life all over again.'

TOM COMES OUT

Oh Monday! Monday!
Oh Monday morning, you gave me no warning
Of what was to be!
Oh Monday morning, how could you leave
And not take me!

Joy sits by her transistor writing to Dave. Jonny runs round the room naked slapping his tummy. A goldfish swims round a small square tank; the water is greenish and a fetid odour rises up from it.

'Saturday morning I go to work and they said in a nice way Joy as you no the weathers getting bad so we will have to cut the staff down until April.

'Well I just exploded. Anyway, I worked Saturday morning, come Saturday night was so chocked it all came on top. I felt so sorry for myself I felt like dying. So now your Joy is no longer a barmaid but I still got the model going well. You know Tom comes out tomorrow. Well I've been up the solicitor and he says dont have him in the house. No I said I dont want him near me. Well Dave *I am going to wait* and I am going to *Marry You* I wont be a nun, but doesnt mean I wont wait you see Dave I KNOW I LOVE YOU, there will never be no one to take your place. May be fasernation but not Love. Dave I do Love you very very much please dont give up for both our sakes (PROMIS) Its not the end of the world its still going round. So chin up Please xx I visit you as much as I can. No one understands you. They think your all bad but I know your not, so that's all that matters.

'I just cant get over that lovely card it was for *me* ME Dave dont never leave me, I need you, you made me feel so wanted, and you made me fille hole what more can anybody want. All we want is to be loved, and feel sicuar? Right xxxx Hears a big kiss. One day I will marry you, and when I get your ring out I wear it for you ... I'm so frighten Whats going to happen to us. Time is such a horrible thing. I always love You Dave for ever you will always be in my heart ... and come home, start a fresh *every day counts* DONT GIVE UP NOT ONE DAY PROMISE.

'God I wish we were settled I'm so mixed up I dont know WHAT I would do without you. Well darling always remmber when your lonely I with you loveing you because your the one I Love, Well darling please write soon. God Bless you and keep you safe and may he help us to face this and bring us out of it. See you soon love.

'We'll have Christmas together one day. Oh well have

children and presents all wrapped up. Oh darling ... I love You. I going to put your card in a fram and put it on the dressing table, Your card means such a lot to me.

'Now dont you *dare* forget to shave every other day. I might come up on the offchance then I might nick you cheating ha ha. Dave I've a confession to make I rinsed my hair Very light brown it looks nice only because I mustnt dye it no more as I've a little rash in it (truth) – I had to do it anyway your like it (I hope) nockout stages anyway I told you ... and on that open visit were have a few ... Sounds marvelose doesnt it, Dave *I've got* to wait for you because your like air, Dave you have made me happy Oh you don't relise how much I need you Dave always. At the moment I have got to be indorpendet, but it will change when you come home, I'll be depending on *You*, and then thats how it will stay. I always want it like that (Yes it is Joysy talking) Dont sound much like her, but in my head (knock knock) there a little Joy that comes out now and again remember when we used to lay in bed and talk about that (the nocks to remmber you before I said it) Oh Dave sometimes I cant think what to say, I just daydream aboat us I wish I could just touch you. Dave on Wednesday 2.30 think of me extray specil because I'll be up the hospital. I frightened Dave. I hope theres nothing wronge with me (No there isnt Joy) xxx I felt you say that, How can I tell you I Love You can you here me Dave saying it. Can You Dave, I can fill you saying it I make myself I believe I can and I close my eyes and there you are. I dont think you let me down, because our love is to preshiose to us. People only have 1 true love, and weve got that so we must cherise it for ever EVER By the way, your have to shrink ha ha I wonder how we used to have it, now it seems so funny your so tall and I'm so small. We musent change because thats *Dave and Joy.*

'Dave I have got a confession to make. When I used to look at men it was to make you jelose, I used to love winding you up – Oh your kill me one of these days. And when you used to look at girls I said I didnt mind, Oh but realy I was fuming. I used to think terrible things in my mind. Oh it wasent jeslose, but love realy. I never wanted to share you either. I dont know in my mind your MINE (Persesive Joysy) ha ha. *Oh Dave* what am I going to do today, its so lovely out, but your not here to share it with me, so I'll just have to watch the film on Tele and have a little sleep.'

Auntie Emm puts the kettle on the gas ring while Joy runs her pink tongue along the back of the envelope.

Joy isn't dressed yet. Her hair is sticking straight out from her head like the branches of dry fern. The fragments of blackened glue cling to her frail eyelids where the false eyelashes have been harshly torn off. Jonny climbs on her knee holding a book. 'Read the book Mum. Here's the book.' 'In a minute my Sweetie, let Mum have a wash first.'

'Remember Emm when I used to have that bike with great big track handles – me mate used to sit on the handlebars. Nowadays I never get no exercise except with blokes, I'm sure that's what's causing me trouble.'

Emm was dying her hair, mixing up a thick reddish black paste and adding boiling water. She had wrapped a tea cloth round her scraggy neck and pinned it with a nappy pin to her pink crepe de chine blouse.

'You want to settle down love, find a man of position.'

'I'm frightened of settling down – it really terrifies the life out of me. When I first married, in two years I only went out nine times. I just lost all interest in life – in everything. That's why I'm frightened of settling down perhaps I'm not destined for security. Some people need change – do you think I'm one of those people?'

Joy poured the rest of the boiling kettle into a bowl and added a drop of cold water. Then she took off her blouse and she soaped up the flannel and she rubbed it down her long white arms and round her narrow neck, wiping her face carefully and washing round her small ears. When she'd finished she rubbed herself dry with the tea towel and re-soaped the flannel in the grey water for little Jonny. 'Come here love, let's have a go at your face,' but he ran and hid behind the kitchen table. She picked him up and sat him on the draining board but he swung his head from side to side. 'Stinky flannel, no, no, no,' he shouted, kicking his bare heels against the sink.

'Don't let anyone tell you what to do or run yer life for yer – you've only got one life you've got to run it for yourself.'

TOM COMES OUT

'Look at his legs Emm, aren't they beautiful?'

'He's got square feet like his mother.'

Jonny stood in the bowl clinging to Joy's head while she tried to wash him. 'Kiss my tummy Mum,' he said pushing her cheek against his belly.

'That kid's going to be all for the women when he grows up.'

'Remember when I went with this Bobby he was ever so nice. When we was out together he always used to say he was my father – really nice I thought that was. And he took me out and he bought me a white dress with emerald green flowers and an emerald green sash, he was a head waiter, he made out he was my father. That was Bob.'

'I'm not half fallin' away Emm – I'm even losin' me tits.'

'The trouble with you is you've been too soft and genuine all your life.'

'Yeah the next bloke I get I'm going to take him on for every penny he's got – if I ever find one with anything worth takin' on.'

The plastic irises in the blue vase, the wedding photo in the Ladbroke-calendar frame on the wall, the plate with the Isle of Man in a little gold map. 'What's the matter with me, I'm a cunt aren't I? I never was a lover of sex in the beginning – it's taken a hold of me.'

Emm stands in front of the mirror, the thick paste on her hair has dried and each bunch sticks out from her head with a silver clip at the end. 'Now time it for ten minutes, please Joy, not longer, remember the colour it went last time when you forgot – the orange in the Spanish flag.'

They laugh. 'Here, I really got a result through that play on the telly last night – he was giving her a tenner every time he had it – some people they don't know what it is to have it hard.'

Emm picks up her false teeth off the draining board and sticks them in her mouth.

'I owe my tallyman fourteen pound. Mind you I had a pair of black tights and they've all shrivelled up, gone all funny.'

There was a loud banging on the door. 'Three knocks Emm, that's us.'

'This time of morning. You go Joy.'

'Frit the blacks out of me that did.'

Jonny ran to the door and Joy picked him up and carried him downstairs. She unlatched the door. There on the step stood Tom.

'You've lost weight,' she said. 'I thought you weren't coming out till tomorrer.'

'No today, trust you to get it wrong. Well aren't you going to let me in?'

'I don't know as I should seeing as there's a divorce proceeding.'

'Let me come in Joy – I want to see Jonny.' Jonny was hiding his face in his mother's neck. She led the way up the stairs.

'Emm it's him – I've said he can have some tea.' On the

landing mad Bet shrieked, 'Men, men, men, always men in there.'

Tom sat on a chair, his face was blotchy from prison, his hands coarsened.

Joy curled her pony tail round her fingers.

'So what do you want?' Jonny still clung to her.

'Hasn't he come on lovely Joy.'

'You make the tea,' said Emm. 'I'm going across for a packet of fags.'

'I met this bloke inside, given me the address of a place out at Catford. Two bedrooms, kitchen and balcony – only three quid a week and in perfect nick.'

'So?'

'Come back with me – give it a try for little Jonny's sake – I'll never lift a finger to you I promise.'

She stood apart from him and watched the tears run down his ugly face.

'I love you Joy.'

'I've got a lot to give up,' thought Joy. She looked round the room. 'At the same time I haven't got a lot to give up.'

The flat out at Catford wasn't too bad, except it was filthy dirty and hospital green in every room.

'It's a filthy place, but I'll soon make it nice – hang up little cottage curtains and you need a bit of lino, say about twenty-five shillings on yer bit of lino, and then you can always collect a bit of second-hand furniture here and there.'

So they spent the first week decorating and Joy made curtains. Tom had a couple of hundred he'd put away before he went in and they lived well.

They went down Shepherd's Bush Market, Joy clutching her plastic bag.

'I want all new stuff for my new flat – I'd like this – oh look at that.' She admired a huge, elongated black-china cat with a pale-pink lampshade poised delicately over its head. 'That's cheap, twenty-three guineas for a veneer cocktail cabinet.'

She filled her shopping bag with shilling packets of plastic toys, and they sat in the open market drinking tea and eating Hamburgers, Jonny between them. She wore her leopard-skin coat and high suede shoes.

And for a moment she is happy.

'Joy, let's go in for another baby. I'll go straight I promise.'

She thought of a baby – a baby girl in a pink frock tottering down the road in a short pink frock with all her little bum showing. 'It might settle me down. I might be an ordinary wife – I'm such a wayward cow.'

Back home she has chopped her bit of carpet into various oblongs and squares to fit the odd shaped kitchen with the sloping ceiling and the skylight and the small square of grey sky.

The front hall smelled of damp, dusty lino – the smell of poverty, of unloved houses which people never live in for very long.

TOM COMES OUT

She thought about the deserted commons, Peckham Rye, Norwood, long-lost land; 'You're not leavin' – you're not leavin' any more.'

An upside-down pram lay in the long grass; a blackbird sat on one of its wheels, cocked his tail in the air and hopped away. At three o'clock in the afternoon it was so still she felt she was going to suffocate ... but she thought of the new child.

I can't stop looking into prams. I can't stop thinking about a little girl – I've only been off the pill since Saturday so I can't have fell yet ... She's going to have everything – the lot, one of them Spanish layettes all lace. Lace around her little hands and a handmade shawl to wrap her in and one of them cradles in pink organdie ... If I train it to be a good baby I can always leave it with me mate. I used to get Jonny off to sleep by singing to him, 'Hush a bye, babby, lie quiet with your daddy' but his bleedin' daddy was never there. I want a white dress with a great big black bow to go over me lump – it'll look terrific with me blonde hair.

I'll hang on to Tom – till someone else comes along or Dave comes out of the promised-land. All I want to do is be happy and contented. I don't want a lot out of life – if I only have six months with Tom and I'm happy – well I've had another six months of happiness. I was a virgin when I went with Tom – mind you I've made up for it since – oh I haven't half had some blokes – even if I have a new baby I can always slip out and no other fucker will know. All I want is to be loved. I wouldn't even mind if Tom went back to thieving – after all it's his life, all he's ever known, really. I don't see no danger, that's the trouble with me. I'm in bed with Tom and I'm having it with him and he says 'If I ever thought another bloke had laid a finger on you I'd kill him and you,' and I think, Oh if you knew – you silly bastard. Well I'm back with him but I won't stay longer than six months – six months of security is the longest I can stick. I'm not going to stop at home all day, I'll have to go out to work. I'll be a barmaid again then I can dress up and look really smart – you've got to be able to dress up to keep yourself going.

A plant like a giant pineapple, with the fruit buried, grew in the desolate garden. Someone had tried to light a bonfire to burn some of the rubbish but it had only burnt the top layer and gone out; beneath was a black and sodden heap of rags and paper and old soup tins, and a child's rubber ring, discarded perhaps when he learnt to swim.

The house faced east, and it was as if the sun had always forgotten to come in.

On the mantelpiece was a wedding anniversary card showing a huge bunch of blue pansies.

> *I want your loving heart to know*
> *My heart belongs to you*

TOM COMES OUT

And on this special day of ours
I want to tell you too
That you are sweet and wonderful
A blessing to my life
And there couldn't be one dearer
Than you my darling wife.

And written underneath: 'To my wife I still love you like allways. Your THE Best Wife in the world Love Tom. Lets have a lot moor years together Darling.' She opened the card and a faint smell of Woolworth's bath salts came out as she pressed her face against the paper.

Tom was up and dressed at seven o'clock, all ready to go to work; he'd got a building job as a cover up. She felt her stomach falling out. 'I fancy it so much, don't go to work.' He got undressed and back into bed.

Later she fried some onions in an empty Fray Bentos steak tin, and they perfumed the air. Then she spread bread with marge and put the soft brown onions between two thick slices. 'Life's one long picnic ain't it, Jonny?' He climbed up onto her knee and together they ate their meal.

'We might as well make plans even if it never comes to anything – all you've got is your dreams that's all life is really, a whole lot of longing what never comes true, eh Jonny?'

She got ready to go out.

'Cor my hair, the things my hair had on it, it must have had every bleeding thing under the sun.'

'It's a sin', she sings.

'Life's so short I'm not going to knock me fucking self out. I haven't made the beds yet, never mind, they can be airing.'

First she sprayed herself all over with body mist – 'It's gone up fivepence in the last month.' And then covered herself in spring-grass talcum powder. Then she put on her all-black undie set with the pale pink ribbon daintily threaded about. 'Pity I ain't still modelling, this would have looked really sexy.'

Next she back-combed her almost white hair and pinned on her false pony-tail, done in her crinoline-lady style.

She walked down the stairs holding rather tight to the banister so as not to catch her spindly heel in the split lino. Pop music poured out of the first-floor flat.

'What now love?' Out of the front door she half tripped, just letting go of Jonny's hand in time, and went flying onto the pavement. Picking herself up, she dusted down her tight skirt and looked up and down the empty street.

'Poor Mum fall down.'

'Never mind love, look at those daffs; first sign of spring, come on I'm going to buy you an ice.' And they walked away together, Jonny running on a little way in front, then stopping to wait while she caught up; so they walked down the deserted road past a wasteland of strewn bricks and dilapidated garden walls, rubbish made into piles and forgotten, and trees, sad and leafless, and garden sheds with broken windows and hopeful birds.

DESOLATION

The vice tightened round her heart, squeezing it with each turn, harder and harder till she felt black with tiredness, claustrophobia and despair. It was two o'clock in the morning and she lay in the big bed alone. Jonny slept in his cot in the corner, she heard his little snores and his every breath was a blow on her aching heart – 'Dave why did you leave me you rotten cunt?'

At about five Tom came in, with a broken transistor radio and two bob in his pocket. He got undressed, not bothering to wash – Joy smelt the grease on his hands. 'I can't crack it, I can't seem to crack it this stretch. All my pals are inside – I keep missing them – when I'm in they're out – now I'm out they're fucking in.'

He fell asleep and snored while it grew light outside the window and Joy lay watching the sky.

'Oh Dave if you'd been with me when he came to the door – if you'd bin by me – why did you fuck off to prison.

I couldn't manage on my own. Oh Dave I've bin so fucking lonely.'

Joy thought of the day she went to the Old Bailey.

It was pouring down with rain, all the way there. And I went in the Court and there's Jonny, poor little sod was crying outside the court while I went in to plead for him and they said ten years and two year contemplative or something like that and I run out of the court and I couldn't breathe – my little Jonny was screaming and I thought my life, my love, they've taken away my whole life and I carried Jonny down the road 'cause he wouldn't walk – he wanted me to carry him. So I carry him down the road in the pissing rain and I don't even feel the wet. Whatever's going to happen to us now, I think, Oh Gawd, if you're really up there, for Christ's sake do something for me.

When Tom got up to go to work he gave her the two bob then walked out of the house, saying: 'When you've got money you've got the best friends in the world. But when you're down and out nobody wants to know.'

She wore an old skirt below her knees and no stockings, her jumper wasn't washed and her hair hadn't been bleached for about a month. She dressed Jonny in his blue jeans – she pulled them up over his square feet shaking him down into them between her knees, then she pulled his red jumper over his head and he changed his tractor from hand to hand as she put his small arms down the sleeves. He was very attached to his tractor and wouldn't go to sleep till the small, red battered object was under the blanket beside him – that and his bottle; although he was nearly three he still liked his bottle. Joy would sit on the settee and Jonny would lie across her knees his head tucked against her breast sucking at his bottle of tea. Together they'd look out of the window at the orange cat and the blue lupins as high as your head in the next door garden.

When I married Tom I loved him. I started again so many times to love him it was such a shock when I realised I didn't love him – when I didn't love his knees and hands and lips and hair. I didn't have it with anybody before Tom got nicked. But Dave brought out what was inside me. I never was a great lover of sex before that, and now I ache for it. But not with him, I can't abear it with him. I feel dizzy when he touches me, I feel sick – I can't abear him – perhaps it's being married.

When you're married to someone they take you for granted, you're there, you're there to come home to, you're tied to the kitchen sink and when you go out, even if you look nice, they never say 'Oh you do look nice' or anything like that, and you sit in a corner all night and that's it. And he'll fuck off and talk to his mates. When you're living with someone it's fantastic. Everything that he does you do. They're so frightened of losing you they've got to keep you satisfied all the time. Dave used to do everything, I never done a thing without him. Honestly, he used to do all my housework – Gospel truth, on my life. He used to do my housework and he did the washing, and he'd go to the baths and ironing, it was fantastic, and we'd very seldom row, he had all the patience in the world. He used to say I spoilt Jonny but he'd never interfere, nothing like that and I lived with him for long enough so I'd know. You can usually tell. People say you can't tell but I can. I was happy with him.

The child across her lap lifted up his leg and touched her cheek with his bare foot. He finished his bottle and threw it across the floor. Joy lifted him off her knees and he ran into the next room to find his toys.

She thought of Shelley – when he took everything off, he had a great pot belly.

The sun came through the skylight as she rubbed down the table with the torn-up rag. The leopard under the television set – she attacked the little scrap of cut up carpet with the carpet sweeper.

I wipe the gas stove down and wash the tray and fill the sugar basin up, after that I get the hoover out and hoover the fucking carpet, then I brush me chairs down and I brood over the row and I listen to the wireless – after that I go in the bedroom and fold all the clothes up then dust down me dressing table. I clean all me stairs down then

I put a bit of Harpic down the lavatory and it's done, then I go down the launderette and get me shopping.

If yer heart's in yer home it's all right, otherwise it's useless.

He comes home last night and he says 'Look who I'm working with, Big Bonzo Hitchins.'

'Who the hell is Big Bonzo Hitchins?'

'Just come out from doing a tenner. Some people have got it in them they can't help it – he'll be in and out all his life.'

I'll have to have some salts, that'll put me right, a big dose of salts.

If I could get rid of him I could go out – have my false piece on top like a cottage loaf. I might win on the spastic shilling-a-week and if you win you can choose anything from a book: Prestige Happymaid; Dish Drainer; a Bex 'Decorair' and four tea towels; Kitchen Timer and Hand Towel; Gents Winter Weight Pyjamas; Six Table mats; Four pairs of gents socks – I'd be well away.

The other night when he got hold of me I thought I was going to spew me heart up. We was watching telly and there was this play and it said, 'I love you Dave.' So I had to distract him so I took me drawers off and lay on the couch. Then when he come to touch me, bang! I'm up in the air. I'm a cunt really I don't know what's the matter with me – it's as if it all came back like on a film. When I came out of hospital and Jonny was only seven days old I had a relapse on the Sunday, I was really ill and I said, 'I do feel ill, Tom, don't go out and leave me.' And he went out and left me.

On the Monday he bought a new suit and I didn't have nothing at all. And he went out and he bought this new suit and dressed himself up. And I was jealous, I told him and he left me. So I thought, Right fuck you, I'll fuck you up one day, I did, I always said dogs had their day. Men are heartless. Women have got more emotional feeling. Men, when their wives are down and out – some blokes who truly love their wives are all right, they sympathise but most just say, 'Oh fuck it,' and walk out and find someone else. When their wives are back on their feet they want them back again. Tom never used to come up every night when the baby was born, like other fathers, with a bunch of flowers or a box of chocolates, nothing like that. He used to come in at twenty past seven and go at half past seven.

He found this letter from a bloke who gave me a box of chocolates – he was the only friend I ever had who wasn't after what he could get. He only phoned him up and called him all the names.

As Beryl used to say, 'Men – they don't think the same way as we do – your trouble is you tell him too much – you should never tell a man anything.'

The yellow plastic daffodils with their dusty frills.

'Me knees – look at me filthy knees – I've bin scrubbing the floor. I painted me toe nails red but I forgot to wipe the dirt off me knees.'

Dishing up the stewed steak, curling at the edges with

gristle – cheap cut – she spills the gravy over her hand and drops the dish. 'Oh fuck me – I'm going barmy scraping potatoes all morning in this poxy hole, it's fucking horrible.'

A great big greasy kettle is on the stove.

'I've got me nerve rash back all up and down me legs itching me.'

The grubby eiderdown with the roses, and she bends to pick the toys up off the floor. She kneels on the lino and tries to sweep under the bed and knocks her head against the table, the lino is cool against her knees.

She looks round the kitchen, the grey formica table and no more letters from Dave.

When I was on my own I liked to go to work and it was like a routine to me. Now I'm all up the spout, I'm fucking all arse upwards. When Tom was away I knew I could do what I wanted to do, but he drags you back. When I told him about modelling, he said, 'No, you don't want that.' Yes, he did, and I give it up. Like a fucking fool. He doesn't know about me in the nude or anything like that. He's seen these other pictures which come out really well, he even said it, but he says, 'You don't want to do that, it goes to your head.' I said, 'It don't go to my head.' What if it does go to my head, anyway? He doesn't want me to go to work. He says, 'All you want is to be amongst men,' but it isn't – I can't get on with women, I don't like women, women are too catty. I mean that's nature. Let's face it. Women get on your wick. They do, on my wick. Going and seeing my mates we have a laugh and all that, but to go and work with other women like in a factory, it'd drive me mad. And at home they start bawling at the kids and things like that, I can't stand that. I spose I could be a brass – if anything happened to Jonny that's what I would do – go professional. It would be terrible. You have nothing. You become numb to everything. You never really think of settling down and having a family, that doesn't ever come into it. You never think of that sort of thing. All you think of is good times and the money. And you find that somebody is going to cut your throat for each penny.

The wind blows almost silently over the wall of the graveyard and up the steps, through Joy's window where she is manipulating an enormous second-hand hoover. There she is out in the wastes of a desolate suburb next door to a municipal graveyard, houses gone downhill, mostly inhabited by blacks, with broken cots and rotting armchairs in the back gardens and bent railings and chipped stone steps in the front. A piece of newspaper blows up and wraps its face around a twisted gatepost which has lost its gate.

When I'm by myself, little Jonny in bed, I just sit and I think of other people who're together. I sit crying and I think of all the times I've had and all the records – I'm very sentimental. If you play a record I think, Oh God, I can remember when I used to be dancing round the floor, Dave with me and I just got to go back. There's a record and it's awful, I even think of when I loved Tom. I think of the *good* times, I forget about the bad, and I think, Oh, what have I done to him? Where did I lack, or I must have lacked as much as he did. I don't always blame it onto him, and I stop crying and think, Well, am I doing the right thing? Am I messing little Jonny's life up? But later it passes off and I forget it.

If I could have made a go with Tom before I met Dave, you see, if I'd never met Dave it would have been all forgotten, it would never have existed, I'd have still been the same Joy to Tom – the same Joy who didn't know no better, who didn't care about sex.

Then again it's not just the sex, it's the closeness – Dave he was so affectionate – kiss and cuddle for hours – but you can't do that so much once yer married – people don't go in so much for kissing and cuddling when they're married. I still sit and cry, when I think of No 8 – the other night I made out that soap got in me bleeding eyes, I was having a bath and all of a sudden it all come back. And I had all tears come to my eyes, I really could feel a lump in my throat like I was going to choke.

'Come on Jonny, let's go out. I haven't made the bed yet but that can be airing. I was ever so particular once upon a time – that was when I was out in Ruislip – but it didn't get me nowhere – so I might as well be rough and ready.'

Jonny jumped down the stairs in front of her, one at a

time, hanging on to the banister railings. He had decided not to hold her hand going down stairs any more ever since she tripped and nearly sent him flying.

A small girl in a knitted bonnet stands in the deserted road – next to an enormous rotting cadillac, the tyres are sunk into the tarmac and the once splendid chrome is covered in dark rust.

'I've always had plenty of people round me,' she thought, 'but I might as well be in China for all the people I ever see out here. He can't go on going to work all day and leave me here on me own I'll go mad. Better to stick to thieving. I said to Tom it's wrong really but he says, "No it's not wrong it's my life. I am a thief that's what I am – I've always been one – a Tealeaf that's me".'

Joy and Jonny sat in the café eating cod and chips, sprinkling the fat chips with vinegar, biting into a roll. The cod encased in a hard cold crust of fat, the dry white flesh of the fish inside and the soft chips cold in the mouth, washed down by warm tea.

Outside the door a dog is being sick in the sunshine; a little girl leans against her mother who talks to another woman.

'I want a pair of them nylon bikini panties, two-and-eleven from the window – not lace-edged, those lace-edged ones don't half catch yer.'

She thought of the last time she'd been to pay the rent.

'I went in and asked him if he'd got any flats, told him I was tired of this one – I had this pink curler in the bottom of me pony tail – he touched it and said, "You've left a curler in Lovey." Oh it was just the way he said it and he touched my hair – oh I do fancy him – I'm going to have him too – come on Jonny.'

They crossed the road – Joy with her skinny, white legs and her Cleopatra hairstyle with the ragged tail hanging over one shoulder, and Jonny clasping her hand, his sturdy little body and thick black hair hanging about his neck in confusion.

Inside, Mr Jacks' office is hung with girlie calendars. Joy pays her rent and then takes down a calendar. 'Do you mind Mr Jacks – I love these girlies – gives me ideas. Oh dear, that's me on a weekend at Brighton, forgotten me nightie.'

Together they flick through them discussing the merits of each girl while Jonny pulls at her skirt wanting to see too. 'She hasn't got enough bust, eh Mr Jacks? I bet you like a girl with plenty of bust.'

Mr Jacks heartily agreed and gave Jonny a sweet. 'Well, Mrs Steadman, I'll see if I can fix you up.'

Joy left cheered by her brief encounter with a man. That's the way to get 'em at it, she thought. I'm going to have him. What did we discuss? Sex. Let's face it that's the only fucking thing to talk about – you can't talk about the rain – it rains every bleeding day. I'd like a flat in Chelsea. Chelsea sounds good. Catford sounds poxy.

They walk across the short burnt grass by the new flats. Women sit in gaudy flowered dresses, hands resting on cheap shiny prams – faces washed and powdered, gossiping of this and that. Little boys in Marks and Spencer shorts run about eating ice cream and ask for more, and fat little girls tumble or sit by, while their mothers talk of slimming and pull in their belts tighter round waists, and worry about the rising cost of washing.

'And did you see the woman who moved into No 14, she's got six kids and all of them spotless – not a mark on them.' And Joy, hearing the chat, is filled with desolation.

How can I go back to all this – I'm not the same any more. I can't stick this sort of security, I can't stick all these women and their kids. I love kids, I'd break the world in half for my Jonny but it's being bogged down every blessed moment and all day among women. You go in the shops, it's bleeding women – you go to the park, it's bleeding women, all so sure, so full of themselves and sex – sex. I can't stand it anymore, when he tried to have it this morning I felt quite dizzy – I screamed at him 'Let me go – let me go you dirty bastard'. I can't abear him to touch me – it's the four walls, the kitchenette, each day the same, I think I'm going round the bend. I'm not like that any more, he wants to make me an old granny pushing a pram – why shouldn't I be a mum and a glamour girl too.

I just want to be something – I can't be nothing all my life. I'm losing everything, I'm even losing me tits. If I wear a short skirt he says I'm showing my legs and if I wear a low dress he says, 'Who are you showing your tits to?' Spose something happened to me like to those people up at the hospital? No one would want me then.

They walked over a bridge and Jonny begged to be lifted up to see the boats, and as she held him on the parapet he pulled down his trousers and peed into the river below. 'Jonny, Jonny,' she was laughing, 'you've no respect – you're always peeing into flower pots, off the platforms of buses, into little girls' dolly prams down every drain we pass – you're as bad as yer mum, you've no respect.'

Jonny laughed. 'I do it again Mum, I do it again.'

'No you don't,' she said. 'Come on we'll have to run or yer Dad'll be home and raving.'

As she came into the flat he shouted at her, 'Where've you been?'

'To pay the rent.'

'Yer a slut you haven't even made the bed – she neglects her home for the sake of a bloke.'

'I went to pay the rent.'

'I know you fancy a bloke in there, you wouldn't bother to go up otherwise.'

A pair of lace drawers are draped over the plastic daffs.

'And where are my tools?'

'I lent them to the bloke downstairs – he come up for a hammer.'

His face went dead white and he sucked in air through his teeth with a great hissing sound. 'You fucking cunt.' His eyes went hard and he hit her across the head, bang, bang; then he hit her in the stomach four times. As soon as he had done it, he grabbed hold of her and started crying. He said, 'What am I doing?' She caught her breath. She couldn't breathe and wanted to vomit. 'Oh you cunt to hit yer own wife and I might be pregnant. Oh you cunt, I'm going.' She ran down the stairs and out of the house. Jonny was sitting in a cardboard box on the steps, a little girl sat next to him in another box, knees bunched up. 'I'm going out darling,' she said, 'see yer Dad if you want anything.' 'Oh I hate him.' Her head was throbbing like a lunatic; a scrap of hair blew across her face as she ran along the road.

Out of sight of the house she began to walk. She remembered camping with Dave by the lake – the trout – fat black-speckled trout lying quiet, still beneath the surface – paddling by the waterfall, rescuing the moorhen from the canal lock – exploring the garden of a deserted house, the flowers growing indoors and outdoors.

An empty-faced woman with red-dyed hair and a narrow gold belt walked along with her poodle and a string bag of potatoes. 'Look at her,' she thought, 'she's been on the game – see her gold belt and gold sandals, she's definitely bin on the game and what's she doing now – she's past fifty and going about with a bleeding poodle dog and a string bag full of potatoes – so you're fucked whichever way you turn.'

From an open window a radio played, 'Take my heart that's all I've got to give. If you don't want me I don't want to live.' A little black girl stood on the doorstep eating an iced lolly. She wore a pink tulle hat and over her arm hung a small plastic handbag.

He won't go, he won't leave me. I can't get rid of him unless he gets nicked, that's why I've got to encourage him to get out and he knows it. 'You just want me to go at it so I get nicked and you can fuck off.'

'You're a terrible fluttery girl, Joy' – that's what they said to me in the pub.

If I was a model they'd do something for me – fatten me up or something, they can change yer whole face and body, tip-to-toe transformation they call it.

I went over Col's and had a couple of glasses of dandelion wine and I was paralytic pissed and I wanted Dave to tie me up and hit me – beat the life out of me.

No man wants to stick to one woman all his life, the ones that do are mugs, Beryl says.

I want so many things – I don't know what I want, I'm so mixed up I don't know what I do want.

If only I could find something worthwhile in life. Now Dave, he made it worthwhile – everything we done together he made it all a treat – even going up the launderette was a laugh. But Tom, if you so much as mention a man at the bus stop engaged you in conversation, he'll say, 'You're always after men, I spose you were looking at him.' He won't even let me wear me false bit of hair, 'trying to get blokes at it,' he says.

At least when I was working in the pub I was someone wasn't I? Everybody knew me – our Joy – they'd call me, Blossom, Sunshine – I meant something to those men. And the men I had it with – even if it was only for me body – well that is me – me body – what else do you expect them to like you for, yer three piece suite?

When they've bin away for some time they get like an animal, all clumsy, they don't know how to handle a woman. Well I've bin used to the best, to men who know what they're up to, I can't abear him banging and crashing all over me.

I wish he'd go at it and get a bit of money, get a couple of thousand and then get nicked.

I can't abear the thought of all these women in the flats around me – all doing the same things – mopping down the lino, washing their husband's shirts, changing their babies, doing the shopping, it's all gone bent on me – the everyday life – the sight of a shopping basket almost turns my guts. If only I had a car – I'd be able to get away – drive off and find somewhere where there weren't no bleeding women with prams – where there weren't no television to sit in front of night after night, and no bleeding husband to clamp down on every little whim that might come my way. I'd drive off in me car and find a place where there were only men and a few glamour girls and flashy clothes and big hotels. But then I'd fuck meself up talking, I always get ballsed up talking to the upper classes. Whoever heard of a girl like me making it?

I suppose my life is over – you only get one chance – it's not that I'm even suffering, I don't really care now I've lost Dave. I only really mind about my Jonny. I can never live with another man, they could never love my Jonny enough. I think of him all the time.

She thought of him asleep, his arms spread-eagled, his mouth open, the empty bottle still inside, his tongue lapping against the teat; the tiny purple veins on his eyelids, his white forehead and the matted black hair twisted over his ears and round his neck.

There's another side of life, where the husband and wife are very happy. My mate, Jackie, she's thirty something, they have it every night, they've got nothing at all. They haven't got a home, nothing, they've got four kids, but they're so wrapped up in each other. When I look at them I laugh, they have their ups and downs but they're so happy. And they'll tell you themselves, they can still have sex and enjoy it, they don't have to dabble in what it's like with other people. This is really what I want, a close intimate life and if I leave Tom – I'm frightened. I'm frightened of being on my own – sposin' I don't find anyone else and ninety-nine per cent of the men I've been with are married and with their wives anyway – so I'd be the odd one out – I can't live on me own and Auntie Emm, well she drives you mad, it's no good living with a woman otherwise it would be one room and National Assistance and Jonny in a day nursery. Drive you up the wall and all she talks about is herself – if I say I think I'm pregnant she lifts up her jumper and says, 'Well look at me – I think I am too' – at her age, fifty-two. I think the world of my Auntie Emm but not to live with. I've got my Jonny and what I feel for my Jonny I could never put in words, but a kid, you want to share a kid, you can't live with a kid alone. When he's out at night I sleep with Jonny in my arms – but it's not really right. Yet I'm frightened I'm so frightened of leaving him – I don't know if I love him – if everything is going easy I'm happy and then kids – if I am going to settle down I must have kids – I mean that's the point of settling down really, isn't it? Either you're out and about having a good time or you make a go of it, have a few kids, a lovely home, that's it, you settle down. But I'm neither one nor the other – I'm not having a good time because he won't let me go anywhere and I can't settle if he's out all night at it – then he comes in in the morning saying he's been at it all night, with one broken transistor worth five bob and I have to go up the Assistance – I try to be honest. I got a great pain in me heart yesterday I really wanted to gas meself. I try to look inside meself and say, is it because you're jealous? You know really he's going with birds when he's out all night – is it jealousy, are you frightened of losing him? Then I think well I've bin with blokes – why shouldn't he have girls – but I can't face it. I've bin with him so long. I've known him since I was about seven – I was at school with him. I started going with him when I was fifteen – I'll never forget that behind the Co-op. Then we got married.

DESOLATION

Six months later little Jonny was born. I've bin with him so long at least I do know him – the blokes I used to go with when I was working at the White Horse, well I could talk to them – I can talk to anyone but it's not the same as your own – and then he's the father of my son and little Jonny loves him. Let the world go haywire, I don't care what happens but don't let no one hurt a hair on my little Jonny's head or I'll take them by the neck and strangle the life out of them.

Then sometimes when he's home, he's good to me, that's another thing. If he were rotten all the time I could go but sometimes for a week at a time he's all over me. I can't do no wrong – I'm a smashing wife – he even lets me wear me pony tail – and I feel a proper mum, I feel great. I go up the park with Jonny and buy daffodils for the table and put a red plastic tulip in the toilet to make it smell nice and the place looks smashing and we're happy again.

Then again you read all this stuff in the papers – result of a broken home – delinquent locked up, all the rest. I don't want my Jonny to be the result of a broken home – if I could find a bloke tomorrow who loved Jonny as much as he loved me I'd go with him.

She walked down the street of tiny houses, the air milky warm when it touched her bare arms and legs. On the door steps were dustbins piled high with rubbish, ready for the dustman in the morning. She looked through a chink in a curtain and saw a young man naked to the waist, a chain around his neck, rocking a baby in his arms. Joy remembered how when he was tiny she had dangled the light bulb over Jonny's head and swayed it to and fro. On bad nights this was the only way she could make him sleep.

On the table were two empty tea cups. The telly was on, wrestlers rolling about the stage like lunatics, but he wasn't watching it, he was looking at himself and the baby in the mirror.

The door opened and a young woman came in. She wore mules on her feet and her legs were slightly bandy in her short cotton skirt. Her long hair was tied by a bit of ribbon. She went up to him, took the baby and sat on the settee. The young man had his back to the window. She could see his muscles move under the bare electric bulb. Looking through the window life seemed so easy – all you needed was a man, a baby and a couple of rooms. That was really what it came to didn't it, someone who loved you really, really loved you and whom with all your beating heart you loved but there was only Dave, and what was she to do for the next twelve years? She thought of him caged up like an ape pacing his cell, like an ape peeing in a bucket, sleeping on a shelf. She thought of him living like an ape while she walked the streets of Catford and the moon shone in the sky, a great round coin of palest gold.

When she got back several hours later the cardboard boxes were abandoned in the moonlight and she went indoors.

'Where's Jonny?' she said to Tom.

He lay on the settee, fat in his vest, watching the boxing on television.

'I thought he went with you.' He took another bite of cake.

'But I told you I wasn't taking him.'

'Here,' he got to his feet and stood in front of her, the clusters of spots on his face were a livid red. 'I'm not a fucking baby-sitter – you look after yer own fucking kid.' Crumbs were sticking to the grease around his mouth. She turned and ran down the stairs calling his name. She banged on the door of Lorraine's house. Lorraine was there, 'bin home for hours – it's after ten, Mrs Steadman.' Couldn't remember where she last saw Jonny – in his cardboard box she thought. Joy felt a panic rising in her stomach and a throbbing in her temples – the flagstones jumped up at her, huge grey blocks as she ran along calling his name. Each garden she looked into but found only broken prams, dog roses and sodden mattresses, the sky was full of stars – she saw him being carried away by a sex murderer, tiny mouth gagged by a maniac's handkerchief. She heard him shriek, 'Mama, Mama.' She ran down an alley, but it was blocked by dustbins spilling over. A headless plastic doll lay at her feet yellow in the full moon.

'My Jonny.' She saw his small, square feet tied together with string, hung from the ceiling, his body dangling upside down in an empty house, his black hair matted with blood.

She saw him in a drawer in the mortuary, already cold from the icy climate.

In one garden was a heap of half-burnt rubbish. Perhaps he'd set fire to himself, and she saw his red sandals among the burnt-out Daz packets and blackened, label-less tins.

She heard his voice, 'Mama, Mama,' and kicked at the door of an empty house. 'Jonny, Jonny,' she shrieked through the window. She cut her hand on some glass and the blood trickled down her fingers. 'What if I don't find him – how could I live without him?' And then over a wall she heard a voice.

'It's a pussycat,' the voice was saying. 'Mama, it's a pussycat.'

'Jonny, Jonny,' she called.

'Mama, come and see the pussycat.'

She ran down the alleyway through a broken door and there she saw him sitting on the ground, his face lit up in the moon-tangled grass, and buttercups over his head, and a black cat on his knees. She held him against her, shaking with sobs.

'Why are you laughing, Mum?' he said.

And she thought then that all that really mattered was that the child should be all right and that they should be together.

'Oh gawd, what a state I'm in,' she said, as, hand in hand, they walked back down the deserted road. 'To think when I was a kid I planned to conquer the world and if anyone saw me now they'd say, "She's had a rough night, poor cow."'